A Murder Mystery Cruise

Dawn Brookes

A Murder Mystery Cruise

A Rachel Prince Mystery

Dawn Brookes

Oakwood Publishing

This novel is entirely a work of fiction. The names, characters and incidents portrayed are the work of the author's imagination except for those in the public domain. Any resemblance to actual persons, living or dead, is entirely coincidental. Although real-life places are depicted in settings, all situations and people related to those places are fictional.

Paperback Edition 2021
Kindle Edition 2021
Paperback ISBN: 978-1-913065-27-0

Cover Images:
Cruise Ship: AdobeStockImages©Romolo Tavani
Magnifying Glass: AdobeStockImages©dlyastokiv
Cover Design: Janet Dado

For my Mum,
I miss you every day.

Table of Contents

Chapter 1

Rachel Jacobi-Prince observed an ostentatious group of people boarding the luxurious *Coral Queen* through the main atrium. She and Marjorie, her octogenarian friend, had come aboard earlier than most passengers after arriving in Southampton soon after lunch. They sat at a small glass-topped table affording them an excellent view of the expansive atrium. This was the hustle and bustle part of the ship where people congregated to enjoy their welcome aboard with glasses of champagne.

An elegant woman about Rachel's height with immaculate white-grey hair caught her attention. The woman, who appeared to be in her late forties, led a group of chic-looking companions. She grabbed Rachel's attention because she reminded her of someone.

"Is that woman a friend of yours?" enquired Marjorie, following her gaze.

"No, but she looks familiar."

"I know what you mean." Marjorie sipped her champagne, watching the group gather round the stylish woman. "Perhaps she's one of those modern celebrities from a reality television show."

"From the way the others are hanging on her every move, she could well be famous," remarked Rachel. "Oh, I've got it now! She reminds me of Meryl Streep when she played Miranda Priestly in the film, *The Devil Wears Prada*."

"I'm afraid I don't watch many films, dear. I am aware of who Meryl Streep is, though, and yes, now you mention it, there is a similarity. Another puzzle solved. Speaking of puzzles, I've arranged a surprise treat for us."

The glint in Marjorie's cornflower-blue eyes sounded warning bells that crashed through Rachel's head. "What does a surprise treat have to do with puzzles?"

Marjorie's twinkle spoke volumes.

"You'd better tell me what it is."

"I might as well, now we're on board and you can't escape. I've been so excited about you accompanying me on a cruise again – especially so soon after your wedding – I couldn't resist signing us up. Now I think of it, though, I'm not convinced it will be your idea of a treat."

Rachel blew out a sigh on two counts. The first one, a reminder of how much she would miss her husband over the next ten days, and the second over what Marjorie had in store for her. She loved her friend and had promised she would join her for the occasional cruise, knowing how much she enjoyed them, but Marjorie could be rash at times.

"Tell me about it."

Marjorie hesitated before cackling. "I've booked us onto a murder mystery adventure."

Rachel's eyes widened and her heart sank. "You're joking?"

The concerned look in her friend's eyes told her it was no joke.

"I imagined it would be fun. We can't possibly come across the real thing again, and you know how much I enjoy helping you solve murders. I thought we could investigate a fictional one." The corners of Marjorie's mouth dropped. "I am sorry if it isn't your thing. I should have realised that with your day job…" Marjorie's voice trailed off.

Understatement of the year! It most certainly wasn't Rachel's idea of recreation. Recent investigations in her day job, as Marjorie put it, and on previous cruises had all involved murder. What on earth had possessed Marjorie to think a murder mystery would be in any way pleasurable?

Rachel gulped a mouthful of champagne. Meeting her friend's concerned eyes, she mellowed.

"Okay, I'll agree to this, but take note, I'm joining you under duress." Seeing Marjorie's head drop, she added, "But you never know, I might learn something."

Marjorie wasn't looking convinced, but joined her in laughter. They clinked glasses. "On the plus side, it involves cocktail parties and inclusive dinners. If we don't like it, we don't have to join in, we can just enjoy the food. It'll be a cinch for us. I love a good murder mystery."

Rachel shot her friend a sideways glance, but something else caught her eye. The Meryl Streep lookalike was arguing with a handsome man who reminded her a little of Carlos. The olive-skinned man appeared younger than Meryl-cum-whoever she was, and she dismissed him with a wave of the hand before turning her back on him. He shook his head and joined an elderly woman, whispering something in her ear.

Rachel eyed the mismatched group and couldn't help staring as they gathered together. There were seven in total, and all but the older woman, who was around Marjorie's age, summoned servers carrying drinks trays. Their gestures were exaggerated, like a group of actors on a stage. Rachel's jaw dropped open. She had a bad feeling about this and looked over at Marjorie, who was enthralled.

"May I ask, Lady Marjorie Snellthorpe, is this murder mystery adventure – as you call it – led by a theatre company?"

"Yes, it is. Murder Mystery Creations is the name. They have excellent reviews. I looked them up on the internet."

Rachel raised an eyebrow.

"Don't look at me like that. I'm not a fossil. Anyway, Jeremy helped me."

Rachel smiled; at least Marjorie and her son were still getting along. They had an up-down relationship, mostly because of his marriage to a demanding and extravagant wife.

She leaned in towards her friend and whispered, "I think that lot might be part of the troupe."

Marjorie's eyes lit up as she took another sip of champagne. "Oh, I do hope so. They're displaying all the qualities of a real-life murder waiting to happen."

Rachel watched the bickering septet for a few more minutes. "Just what I was afraid of." She closed her eyes.

***

The welcome cocktail party for the murder mystery adventure, aptly titled 'Murder on Deck', was already lively when Rachel and Marjorie arrived. Rachel felt relief on seeing so many other guests in attendance – she'd been dreading it being a small group of six or seven – and was even more relieved that it wasn't fancy dress. She would have looked it up on the internet, but had spent too much time talking to Carlos before they sailed, then had to rush to the safety drill before racing back to her suite and dressing for dinner. At least she was in the luxury suite at the rear of deck fifteen. She wouldn't be able to afford the luxury on her police salary, but Marjorie always took the one on the port side and insisted Rachel have the one on the starboard side. Rachel hated taking advantage of

Marjorie's wealth, but there was no point protesting. It was a battle she couldn't win. Even Jeremy approved and told Rachel not to worry about it.

"She doesn't spend much on herself, and she appreciates you going with her. So do I, as a matter of fact." Marjorie's son hated cruises and was happy to pass on the task to Rachel, who loved them and enjoyed spending time with Marjorie.

Marjorie's eyes shone when she entered the Cocktail Lounge on deck six, where they were meeting for Act One of their 'treat'. Immaculately turned out in a light grey cocktail dress with her freshly permed snow-white hair accentuating her dainty features, Rachel's friend looked stunning. With Marjorie being much smaller than Rachel's five foot ten inches, she had to look up at most people.

"So many people! This is going to be such fun. Come on, Rachel, let's get a drink."

They didn't need to look far, as a stocky man wearing black trousers and a bright white coat appeared from nowhere with a tray laden with drinks and canapés.

"Would you like cocktails, ladies?"

"Oh, yes please," answered Marjorie. "What do you have?"

"Alcohol or non-alcohol, ma'am?"

"Oh, alcohol, please."

"We have the Mai Tai, a rum cocktail, tonight, ma'am, or champagne."

"I'll have a Mai Tai, then." Marjorie took the full glass topped with cherries, mint leaves and a slice of lime. Rachel helped herself to the same drink from the tray the server held towards her. Taking a sip, she coughed and scrunched up her eyes.

"Wow! That's got a kick to it."

"I think it's the curaçao," Marjorie remarked.

The server nodded his agreement. "You know your drinks, ma'am." He chuckled as he moved to the next gathering.

"Sarah would like this drink. Rum's her second choice after Pernod."

"Where is Sarah? I haven't seen her since we boarded."

"I expect she's on duty. They do a surgery about now, don't they? I called her this morning, and she said she'd come and find us when she got away. Sailing days are always busy for the medical team."

"Yes, especially on turnaround days, as they call them." Marjorie giggled. "I bet she doesn't know what we're up to."

Rachel frowned, knowing Sarah would disapprove, but saying nothing.

"Shall we mingle?" suggested Marjorie.

The Cocktail Lounge was becoming busier and the volume of chatter increased as people availed themselves of the all-inclusive cocktails. Rachel realised this adventure must have cost Marjorie a fortune. She took her arm.

"Thank you for the surprise, I'm sure it will be entertaining. Let's find out who our fellow sleuths are."

As they made their way through the milling crowd, Rachel found herself being drawn in by the atmosphere. She wondered how it would all pan out. She spotted the Meryl Streep lookalike giving directions to crew members and caught sight of the assistant cruise director, Tatum Rodman, standing nearby, chatting to passengers.

Marjorie found two women, possibly mother and daughter, standing by themselves, holding champagne glasses. "Are you looking forward to a good murder?" she asked, chuckling.

"Can't wait," replied the older of the two, a woman in her fifties with shoulder-length auburn hair. "We do these all the time back home. First time we've joined one on a cruise, though. Myra's branching out."

"Who's Myra?" Marjorie asked.

The younger woman explained. "Myra's the owner of the Murder Mystery Creations. They put on the best murder mysteries we've experienced, and we go to a lot. Mum loves them. I'm Kate, by the way. Mum's Enid."

Marjorie shook hands with both women. "I'm Marjorie. Pleased to meet you, and this is Rachel – a dear friend."

Rachel caught the exchange of glances. "I'm Marjorie's adopted granddaughter." She didn't bother to explain how they had met when she'd saved Marjorie from a hitman during her first cruise.

"Is Myra the woman Rachel thinks looks like Meryl Streep?"

"From *The Devil Wears Prada*?" Kate laughed. "I agree, she has a certain resemblance; not only in looks, either. She's a stickler when it comes to putting on the shows. Oversees every detail. She has an assistant manager, but he's more of a dogsbody if you ask me."

"I'm sensing even more friction this time," remarked Enid, glancing over to where the woman called Myra was having heated words with a man who looked to be in his forties. Rachel wondered if he could be the assistant manager or dogsbody Kate referred to.

"It must be the pressure. This is a trial run, Demos told me." Rachel noticed Enid's cheeks flush at the mention of the name.

"Yes. If this one goes well, they'll get a regular, rather lucrative contract." Kate added.

"Who's Demos?" asked Rachel.

"Demos Benedict. He's that gorgeous hunk over there."

Rachel and Marjorie followed the direction of Kate's eyes. It was the man Rachel had seen arguing with Myra after boarding. She studied him more closely. Six foot with black hair, a neatly trimmed beard and moustache, thick eyebrows and a physique to die for.

"Is he Italian?" He reminded her so much of Carlos, except Carlos didn't have the facial hair.

"No. He's half Greek, half English," said Enid.

"How do you know that, Mum?"

Enid blushed again. "We were chatting during the Bath Murders a few weeks ago."

"He is rather handsome," remarked Marjorie.

Rachel studied both women's reactions to the actor and suspected they each had a crush.

"Are there always so many people?" she enquired.

"At the murder mystery weekends, there are often around one hundred to one hundred and fifty of us," Enid replied. "This one's a bit smaller, I'd say. I recognise some people, though."

"And a lot more expensive," Kate remarked. "The weekends are pricey enough, but add a cruise on top – some people just couldn't afford it, I suppose."

Rachel glanced towards Marjorie, troubled at having her suspicions over the high cost confirmed. Marjorie was too busy looking over at the formidable Myra to notice.

"She likes to dish out the orders, doesn't she?"

"There's no mistaking who's in charge, if that's what you mean," laughed Kate. "Myra Slade. Some regulars have nicknamed her Myra Blade because of the sharp tongue. I'd hate to work for her, but she puts on a great show. Is this your first murder?"

Marjorie choked on her drink, causing the two women to stare at her. Rachel intervened before her friend revealed she was a CID detective.

"It's the first time we've attended anything like this, that's for sure."

There was no time to say anything else, as the sound of the microphone sparking into life brought the gathering to attention.

Chapter 2

Tatum Rodman, the assistant cruise director, introduced herself, welcoming everyone aboard the *Coral Queen* and waxing lyrical for ten minutes about all the activities passengers could avail themselves of. When she finished her spiel, she introduced Myra Slade who, up to that point, had been tapping her foot impatiently. The other woman forced a smile and grabbed the microphone.

"Good evening, ladies and gentlemen, I hope you're looking forward to our maiden cruise-ship performance. My name is Myra Slade, owner, founder and director of Murder Mystery Creations offering unique crime conundrums where you, the observers, get the chance to solve the murder, or murders. As part of your cruise holiday experience, we will entertain and bamboozle you with a wonderful cast of actors and actresses. In keeping with our holiday theme, and because this is our first cruise venture, we've set the scene on board a cruise liner. The creation is entitled 'Murder on Deck' and is set in the 1970s. In keeping with the era, we ask you not to use mobile phones at all during the performances. Remember, they were not available in the 70s."

A ripple of laughter filled the room, drawing a huge grin from their hostess. Rachel had already gleaned the title from the notice board at the entrance.

Myra paused before continuing with her introduction. "I hope you enjoy the challenge of unravelling the mystery set before you over the next few days."

Rachel frowned at the mention of a few days, but decided she'd just have to go with the flow. Passengers applauded while Myra introduced a small cast of actors, some of whom had been pointed out to Rachel and Marjorie by Enid and Kate earlier. Demos Benedict drew large hollers of appreciation from many of the women present, earning them a glare from Myra. Enid and Kate competed with his new fan club to be among his loudest.

Next to be introduced was a short, rotund woman called Nellie Hurst with a bleach-blonde bob.

"She's been to a Botox clinic," whispered Marjorie into Rachel's ears.

"What good eyesight you have, Marjorie," Rachel quipped back.

"How old would you say she is?"

"I don't know. Early sixties?"

The next two members of the cast to be introduced were a Leanne and Dudley Bates, Dudley being the man Myra had been arguing with not long before.

"He's the assistant manager," shouted Kate, vying against the noise of the applause, confirming what Rachel had suspected. "She never uses his title when introducing him, though."

After the introductions, Myra explained there would be sessions over five evenings. Each would start with cocktails followed by dinner and drinks, followed by a thirty-minute performance.

"You will witness a murder during the first performance tonight. Act One will take place on the fictional deck of a luxury cruise liner just like this one," said Myra. "We give all attendees the opportunity to watch repeat performances via an exclusive channel on your stateroom televisions. If you miss a performance or want to recap, I suggest you take advantage of the reruns. Especially if you want to win the prize of an evening in a royal box at the Coral Theatre with a bottle of champagne and a box of luxury Belgian chocolates. You may question our cast of suspects after each performance and whenever you come across them around the ship. The team is working, so please feel free to speak to them as often as you like until the final performance."

"Five evenings!" whispered Rachel while passengers were focusing on Myra's spiel.

"Yes. It's all in the brochure," Marjorie replied gleefully.

"Great!" Rachel muttered.

"We convene for dinner in an hour's time. Please sit in groups of no less than four and no more than eight. Experience has shown these group sizes to be the most productive. Thank you. We'll see you in an hour."

Myra waltzed off the stage to rapturous applause, taking the hand of a man of similar age and whispering something in his ear. His cheeks reddened. Myra hadn't introduced the man as one of the cast.

Perhaps he's her husband.

"Do you mind if we join with you two?" Enid asked. "I find four's enough, otherwise people's concentration wanders and they don't pay attention."

"We'd like that, wouldn't we, Rachel?" Marjorie answered.

Rachel nodded approval. "So we're eating in the Cocktail Lounge?" She noticed crew and staff moving tables around, setting them up strategically with a view of the stage. Her hopes of quality time with Marjorie and meet-ups with Sarah were being dashed to pieces, her one consolation being 'Murder on Deck' was only for five nights out of ten.

Glancing over at the Creations crew, she wondered how they had got together. Myra's likely husband or partner appeared out of place, aloof from the others. She would study the brochure as Myra's introduction had been perfunctory at best, probably only concentrating on the principal characters. Presumably they would get a programme or scene sketch over dinner.

"Who's that intellectual-looking man with the paunch?" Rachel asked, nodding towards the outcast.

"I don't know," said Enid. "He's not a regular, unless he's recently joined. He looks a bit too shy to be an actor, doesn't he?"

Exactly what Rachel was thinking.

"I don't recognise the older woman, either. They must both be new."

Rachel had noticed the older woman earlier in the day, shortly after boarding. She appeared confident and comfortable in her surroundings.

Marjorie took her arm, interrupting her musings. "Shall we track Sarah down after the show?"

"Oops! No need." Rachel nodded her head towards the frame of her best friend, stunning in her officer whites, pulling along her medical bag on wheels. Sarah headed towards the side of the stage. "She must be on call."

Enid and Kate were engaged in conversation with a couple of male passengers, so Rachel and Marjorie shifted themselves through groups of people to find out where Sarah was heading.

"Oh, it's one of the Creations troupe, the old girl," Marjorie declared.

Sarah attended the older woman Rachel had just been talking about with Enid. The shy man who she thought might be Myra's husband spoke earnestly to Sarah. Rachel craned her neck, but couldn't hear what was being said.

After checking the woman's blood pressure and giving her a tablet, Sarah took an exit. Rachel seized the opportunity and raced after her. Once outside in the corridor, she called out.

"Sarah!"

Sarah spun around, beaming as she rushed towards Rachel. The two women hugged.

"I called both your rooms earlier, but you must have already left. I'm on call tonight, but can meet you for breakfast tomorrow… hang on a minute. Where did you just come from? Don't tell me you're part of our murder mystery event?"

Rachel frowned. "Marjorie's idea of a treat."

Sarah's jaw dropped open. "You're kidding!"

"That's what I said when she told me; I wish I was joking. Still, the holiday's all about Marjorie's convalescence, and 'Murder on Deck' only lasts five nights."

Sarah rolled her eyes, then smiled. "Corny title, isn't it? They're putting on two of these with a different victim and murderer in each. Otherwise, the story's basically the same. You're in the first group, then. The second's for the latter half of the cruise."

"Glad we're in the first batch; at least I'll enjoy the second half of the holiday. Actually, that's not fair; from what I've seen so far, it could be fun."

Sarah raised an eyebrow.

"Well, maybe not fun, but the food and drink will be enjoyable. One actor reminds me a bit of Carlos. I thought he was Italian, but he's half Greek."

"You'd better stay away from him, then. I don't want you transferring your affections over to some Carlos lookalike."

Rachel laughed and slapped her friend on the arm. "No chance of that."

"The murder mystery thing is something new the cruise director wanted to try. Tatum knows the owner of this mob, so she recommended them to him."

"Tatum's the assistant cruise director, isn't she? She introduced the evening. How does she know Myra Slade? Also a lookalike, by the way."

"Yes, Tatum was new when you and Carlos took your honeymoon, and I'm not sure how they know each other. Who does Myra Slade look like, then?"

"Meryl Streep."

"Mm. Well, she's a force to be reckoned with from what I hear. I hope they will not be too demanding, Bernard's already had one callout to deal with the same woman I've just been to."

"Is she ill?"

"Hypochondriac according to Bernard, but judging by what I've just observed, she's attention seeking because she's not happy her son's going out with Myra."

"How did you glean all that information in the space of five minutes?"

"I didn't, Graham warned us about her at a briefing this afternoon. Her name's Gladys Knott. She's a retired consultant neurologist and wrote ahead with a list of her medical requirements, none of which warranted the senior medical officer's attention at all."

"Poor Dr Bentley. How come you got away so quickly?"

"Because I'm a lowly nurse. Besides, I told her Dr Bentley would make a stateroom visit first thing in the morning. She lapped it up."

"But how do you know her son's dating Myra Slade?"

"Tatum. Apparently, she's also had a recent affair with another man in the troupe. Can't remember his name, but I know he's married to one of them. All a bit incestuous if you ask me."

"It can only be Dudley Bates, the assistant manager. The other guy's too young for her, and I'm assuming the Knott woman's son is the one who was hovering around like a frightened chicken while you examined her." Rachel lowered her voice. "I've heard and observed that Myra treats Dudley like dirt."

"It appears I'm not the only one with inside information, then. Anyway, Dr Knott's son – yes, the one clucking around – seems nice enough. Henpecked, though, and unmarried at fifty. I suspect Gladys Knott has had plenty to do with that fact."

"There you are." Marjorie appeared from behind them. "Hello, Sarah."

"Hello, Marjorie, you look well; it's lovely to see you," Sarah leaned down to kiss Marjorie's cheek.

"Has Rachel been telling you about our new adventure?"

Other guests who had left were returning to the Cocktail Lounge and the corridor they were standing in, although wide, was filling up fast.

"Yes, she has, and I have to say, you're incorrigible, Lady Snellthorpe."

Marjorie ignored the mention of her title, something she didn't like to draw attention to – unless it might help solve a case.

"I discovered it in the activities brochure a few weeks ago, and couldn't resist booking us on. I imagined it would be fun, but sometimes I forget that Rachel sees enough of murder in the CID. I can be a batty old woman at times."

Rachel took Marjorie's arm. "The cocktails are something else, though, and I expect the dinners will be scrumptious."

"I do hope they make up for my faux pas. I take it you're working, Sarah?"

"Yes. I was just asking Rachel, can we meet for breakfast tomorrow? There's only one sea day before our first stop, and the forecast's good considering it's autumn. I'm hoping I won't be too busy tonight. The team told me to send their love when I saw you. Graham was going to invite you both to the officer's dining room for dinner tomorrow, but I'll tell him you're otherwise engaged. It'll be the talk of the medical centre." She winked at Rachel.

"Well, tell him he's not off the hook; we'll take him up on that offer later in the week." Marjorie grinned.

"I'll pass on the message. Catch you both in the morning. Would 8am in the buffet suit?"

"Perfect. See you then." Rachel hugged her friend again and took Marjorie's arm before heading back to the Cocktail Lounge for Act One.

Chapter 3

Food aboard the *Coral Queen* was always of the highest standard, and tonight was no exception. Rachel ate as much as she could, realising she hadn't eaten since breakfast. Marjorie's chauffeur had driven them to Southampton, and when they stopped for lunch on the way, Rachel wasn't hungry. Missing Carlos, this being the first time they were going to be apart since their honeymoon, she had settled for coffee while Marjorie tucked into a Caesar salad. Once dinner aromas filled the Cocktail Lounge, she realised just how hungry she was.

She pushed the last bowl away and sipped at her coffee. "That was wonderful."

Marjorie looked at her. "I could see you were enjoying it; you've hardly said a word over dinner. Enid and I thought you hadn't eaten for a week."

Rachel's cheeks burned as she felt her face flush. "Sorry. Did I miss anything?"

"We were talking about the Creations crew."

It appeared they would refer to Murder Mystery Creations by its shortened version from now on. "And?"

"Nothing much, just mentioning the two new ones. Enid and Kate haven't seen them before. The older woman – she looks about my age, perhaps a bit younger – and the rather clumsy-looking fellow. When I say clumsy, I mean odd one out, really. The one you asked about earlier. He doesn't seem to fit, somehow."

"That's because he's not an actor and the older woman is his mother. He's dating Myra. She must have roped him in to be part of the cast. I can't envisage him having a speaking part, though."

Kate's eyes widened. "How did you find all that out? You were only asking about him just before dinner."

Not wanting to tell them that Sarah had told her, Rachel improvised. "I heard someone mention it when I was outside in the corridor."

"Now I see why Dudley's so put out," said Enid. "Demos told me he and Myra were having a fling behind Leanne's back."

Now it was Rachel's turn to drop her jaw, not at the revelation, as Sarah had already told her, but at Enid knowing about it.

"Which one is Dudley?" asked Marjorie. "I've lost track."

"The tall guy with the ponytail. The assistant manager and married to Leanne, the fierce one over there," answered Kate, pointing towards the woman Myra had introduced.

"Now I know who he is," said Marjorie. "I saw him arguing with the woman you've just pointed out as his wife. I'm afraid I took a micro nap when they were being introduced – apart from when the dashing Demos drew such hysteria, that is. I'm not good with names."

Rachel sat back thoughtfully. With all the tension in the troupe, it amazed her they managed to work together at all. On top of that, Myra was obviously less than discreet about her affairs, so Dudley's wife must have known about it.

"Perhaps putting on a murder mystery helps dispel their anger," she mused out loud.

Enid, who was finishing her coffee, paused midway. "You know, you make a good point which makes perfect sense. I've often wondered how they manage to put on such amazing performances, I think you've nailed it. It's not just the ones on board today who bicker. They all do from what we've seen, although…"

"Although what, Mum?" asked Kate.

Enid sighed. "They seem to have ratcheted up the tension. Even Demos doesn't look his happy self."

"He shouldn't have told you about the affair, though. He can be indiscreet." Kate turned to Rachel. "Although I'd forgive him anything if he bought me a drink."

Rachel noticed a flicker of a frown cross Enid's face. Hopefully, neither woman would have to choose between the hunky Demos or each other.

"He strikes me as a ladies' man. All those women crowing over him when he was introduced, anyone would think he was a rock star. I don't think some of the male passengers were too happy about it," remarked Marjorie, who didn't seem to have picked up on the pheromones oozing from mother and daughter towards the man in question.

"I believe some men were just as enthusiastic," laughed Rachel.

The servers cleared their table and brought a bottle of wine for Enid and Kate before turning to Marjorie and Rachel.

"Drinks, ladies?"

"I'll have a brandy, please," Marjorie answered.

"Martini and lemonade for me, please," said Rachel.

Enid and Kate excused themselves to go to the Ladies, so Rachel took her opportunity. She whispered to Marjorie, "I think they both have a thing for Demos."

"Oh," Marjorie lowered her voice in response. "I gathered Enid did, but I didn't notice Kate had too. I don't think we need worry; he'll be taking up with some rich young thing, I expect. There are plenty to choose from around here."

Rachel glanced around the room, which oozed extravagance and wealth, although the average age must have been around sixty, so youth was a matter of perspective. Marjorie was born to money and her husband had been wealthy, leaving her his business. Although her son Jeremy ran it, Marjorie owned it. Carlos did private investigative jobs for them occasionally; he had been working for Jeremy when Rachel first met him.

"Perhaps Enid's rich," she mused aloud. "Why else would a man in his thirties endear himself to her?"

"She's rather attractive if you ask me. Some men like a more mature woman. Anyway, she's not old, mid-fifties at most."

Rachel contemplated Enid and agreed with Marjorie: she was appealing and distinguished. Her stylish dress sense, although attractive, didn't boast wealth or extravagance. Her face was framed well by the light reddish-brown hair that fell in waves around her shoulders, adding to her appeal.

"Guileless?"

Marjorie nodded. "I was trying to think of the word, you're right. There's an innocence about her which many men would find attractive. Kate, on the other hand, is pleasant, but rather plain by comparison."

Rachel nudged her as the two women returned to the table. Shortly afterwards, their drinks arrived and the room came to a hush. The show was about to begin.

The lights dimmed around the room, except for those aimed at the stage where the actors were in position to perform their first act. Wall-mounted television screens flickered into life; the performance was being live-streamed for people who didn't have a direct view of what was happening. Rachel and her company were close enough not to need them, but the room extended quite a way away from the stage.

The show started with an informal dinner party. The acting was reasonably high quality and the props had been set against a huge scenic backdrop with a picture overlooking the sea, as if the actors were on the deck of a real cruise ship. Rachel was right about Myra's boyfriend not having a speaking part; he played the role of a waiter serving drinks to the guests. His mother, however, played a leading part. The Duchess Christine Bloom was self-indulgent, dishing out orders and insults to all and sundry. She acted the role well, and Rachel suspected it wasn't too far away from the true Gladys Knott. Myra had cleverly cast people in roles they were likely to shine in.

The central story revolved around a dysfunctional family getting together, with petty rivalries, bitter arguments and the odd affair: all quite entertaining and amusing at intervals. Marjorie chuckled all the way through, although Enid and Kate kept their eyes fixed firmly on Demos, who played the part of the duchess's grandson, Sly Toner. Sly's attendance at the family get together was a compulsory part of inheriting his share of her fortune.

Following a deluge of bickering with insults batting back and forth, frenzied activity took everyone by surprise.

Dudley Bates, playing the part of Marvin Black, a spoilt and washed-up 1970s rock star, grabbed hold of Nellie Hurst, playing the part of a lounge singer called Toni Cleeves. Toni screamed as he pulled at her, thrashing about. She pushed him away, terrified, and he dropped the champagne glass he was holding before falling to the floor. All the actors rushed to Marvin crumpled up on the floor while Sly Toner shouted they should call for help.

The stage curtains closed.

Raucous applause filled the room and people stood in appreciation.

"So realistic," shouted Marjorie above the din to nods from Enid and Kate.

"I told you they were good," Enid called back.

No-one but Rachel seemed to think the performance and scream were too realistic. Her heart sank when she heard frenetic activity behind the curtains.

***

Moments after the final curtain closed on the scene, loud music transmitted through the Cocktail Lounge.

"That's strange," remarked Enid. "They generally come out to take a bow and give us instructions on what to do next."

"I overheard a lot of commotion backstage," said Kate. "They must have a technical glitch; it is their first time on a ship, after all. I suspect Myra's not got as much control over sound and stuff as she likes to have." Mother and daughter soon forgot about the curtain call, laughing together and ordering more drinks.

"Well, I suggest it's time Marjorie and I got some fresh air." Rachel rose from her seat, picking up her evening bag, catching Marjorie's eye with a silent warning not to argue.

"What a good idea. As much as I enjoyed our introduction to murder on a cruise ship, a breath of fresh air would be nice. All we have to do now is work out whodunnit." She winked at Enid. "Goodnight, ladies. Do enjoy the rest of your evening. Same time and place tomorrow?"

Kate raised her empty glass. "We look forward to it and we'll compare notes over dinner."

"Quite," said Marjorie, getting up from the table, frowning towards her unfinished brandy.

Rachel tried to hurry away from the crowds exiting the lounge. It was hopeless; Marjorie's pace wasn't what it used to be and numerous groups of people blocked the exits, making it slow going. She could tell Marjorie was itching to ask why they'd left in such a hurry, but it was enough for her to negotiate around the masses.

Rachel took her friend's arm and whispered, "Let's go to battle headquarters."

Marjorie's eyes lit up and she instantly accepted that Rachel meant the Jazz Bar. This was one of their favourite haunts where they had discussed cases in the past. The only thing Rachel didn't know was whether Marjorie suspected her reason for wanting to leave or whether she believed it was so that the two of them would have the edge over the others.

"Don't tell me you've worked it out already," Marjorie answered the unspoken question as they found a booth at the back of the Jazz Bar.

"No, but I suspect there may have been an 'actual' murder. Didn't you hear the commotion Kate mentioned after the show?"

"I can't say I did. The applause went on for ages. I'm amazed you heard anything at all."

"It was the look on the actors' faces, and then the bustling and shouting afterwards. I wasn't sure if it was part of the act or whether something else was happening."

"Rachel, perhaps they are just good at what they do; they are actors, after all. You're letting your imagination run away with you. I'm pleased you're taking it seriously, though. I knew you would enjoy it once the whole thing got started."

"Marjorie, whilst it was a passable—"

"I'd describe it as excellent."

"Okay, good performance, trust me when I say something unexpected happened. You were there when Enid said they usually take a bow and so on. When did you last go to a show without a curtain call?" Rachel's irritation caused a momentary flicker of hurt to appear on her friend's face. "Sorry, I didn't mean to snap."

Marjorie thought for a moment. "Whilst I have every confidence in your instincts, it could have been – as Kate suggested – a technical hitch. The noise you heard could equally be the actors letting off steam after the show; we've already seen how excitable they can be."

Rachel had to consider that what Marjorie said made sense, and now she was away from the tense atmosphere the show had created, it seemed less likely anything was amiss. She ordered drinks from a waitress who arrived at their booth.

"Martini and lemonade for me, and I suspect a brandy for my friend?"

"Yes. A brandy for me, please." The waitress left to get their drinks.

"I can't be certain, Marjorie, but I thought I heard Dr Bentley's authoritative tone."

"I concede someone could have taken ill again. Perhaps it was the Knotted woman Sarah attended to earlier." Marjorie smirked at her name mashup. "She is rather old to be playing a lead role; I expect the excitement got to her. I still think you're reading too much into it."

It surprised Rachel her friend wasn't revelling in the fact that there might well be another crime to investigate, but she was still recuperating from her pneumonia bout, so perhaps a fictional murder was all Marjorie could cope with.

"I suppose you're right, I must be getting ahead of myself. Maybe it was a technical hitch or someone took ill.

I can't even be sure it was Dr Bentley I heard. There was a lot of noise, as you say."

By the time their drinks arrived, the smooth sound of jazz was filling Rachel's ears, relaxing her. She dismissed her earlier trepidation and told herself she was indeed getting carried away.

"Now, though, we do have to think about what we saw and try to solve the murder. That rascal Don Bates played deserved to die, if you ask me. He was only after the duchess's money, after all – a nasty man, and a drunk at that."

"Now who's taking it all too seriously? And it's Dudley, not Don."

"Really? I could have sworn it was Don. He looks so like a Don, don't you think?"

Rachel laughed. "We can rename him if you like."

Marjorie chuckled. "What was the name of the character he was playing?"

"Marvin Black."

"You really were paying attention!"

"You know I can't resist a good, clean murder," Rachel smiled. "Anyway, I read the programme on the table when I got bored. Here. It has a list of characters. Remember, Dudley's the assistant manager who had a fling with Myra. Judging by the daggers his wife was shooting him throughout the evening, both in and out of role, I'd say she knows all about it."

"You miss nothing, do you?"

Rachel sighed. "Sometimes I wish I did miss things, but I guess it's what makes me a good policewoman."

Marjorie took the two-page programme, which sketched out a brief summary of who was who. "Ah, his wife was playing the duchess's sister, Dora Michaels. She played her part well. Caustic, wasn't she?"

"Yes, she was. They were all pretty good in their roles, and it was a believable plot."

Looking up from the brochure, Marjorie added, "I don't like the name Marvin, it reminds me of an old business associate of Ralph's. He was an unpleasant fellow, too. We'll stick to Dudley."

"Right."

"Or Don." Her friend winked. But while Marjorie read the programme, Rachel couldn't shake away the feeling in her gut.

Chapter 4

Sarah finished seeing to a passenger who had sustained a gash to her elbow after stumbling into one of the casino card tables. She glued the deepest part of the gash together and applied antiseptic cream to the remaining area.

"There you go, Mrs Henshaw, good as new."

"I still think I should get a tetanus shot," slurred the inebriated woman.

"You're bang up to date with tetanus shots; in fact, you've had more than those recommended for a lifetime." Sarah repeated the information she'd already given. "Had the card tables not been professionally polished, I would give you a much more painful shot of gamma globulin."

"Whatever you say, sweetheart." Mrs Henshaw ushered herself unsteadily out of the treatment room, her husband helping her when she got to the waiting room. Sarah went into one of the clinic rooms to finish entering her notes on the computer.

Janet Plover, the recently appointed junior doctor, popped her head around the door. "Everything all right?"

"Yep, another inebriated passenger's wound dealt with. It's been relatively quiet. How about you?"

Janet was on emergency call from the doctors' side of things, but Sarah would deal with most of the callouts as the team took turns in having a lead on-call person. They helped each other out whenever they could. Janet was a breath of fresh air after the sudden departure of Brillo Sin, an unpleasant medic whom the whole team… no, the entire ship was glad to see the back of.

From the moment Janet arrived, there had been a pleasant change of atmosphere. A five-foot nine-inch Welsh bundle of energy whose sense of humour was infectious, she was fun, outgoing, helpful and, more importantly, competent. She was older than Sarah and recently divorced, or liberated as she called it. The medical team was back to being a cohesive and supportive group of people.

"Busy enough, but not too busy. Only two callouts after surgery. Not bad for boarding day."

She laughed and Sarah joined in. "Yes, some passengers are under the impression they have to drink us dry on the first night."

"Do you fancy a coffee? Gwen left that fancy machine of hers on for us because we were both seeing people."

"I'd love one. Then I need to eat, I'm starving."

"Me too. Where are you heading?"

"I was going to the buffet. Shall we go together?"

Janet scrunched her freckled nose. "Erm… would you be happy if we went somewhere else?"

Sarah cackled. "I've yet to introduce you to our friend, Lady Marjorie Snellthorpe. She isn't a fan of the buffet, either, so you and she will get on so well. My best friend Rachel frequents the buffet, and she's a fitness fanatic. There are healthy options, you know?"

They walked into senior nurse Gwen Sumner's office to gather their coffees.

"I can't wait to meet them both. Everyone says Rachel's a murder magnet, but I still think you're all having me on with those stories! And I have to point out that, as I'm a member of the fat, fit and fabulous club, it's not the food I have a problem with. I'm a germ-aversion freak, and despite the generous amounts of hand gel scattered around the ship, I would need to wear full body armour to venture back in the buffet after my one and only experience for my own safety."

Sarah bent over double, laughing at the empowering description of Janet's body and the accurate observation of the scrum that was the ship's buffet sometimes. When she finally recovered, she countered, "You just need to know the quietest times, but I will concede that you would have to touch a serving spoon someone else will have handled.

So rather than put your life at risk, what say we compromise? How about the officer's dining room?"

Janet handed Sarah a mug of coffee. "Now you're talking." Her big brown eyes shone with humour as she flicked back the wavy red hair that fell in front of her face.

Yep, she really is a breath of fresh air.

"On another note, have you seen Graham this evening? They called me to see his latest challenge – the woman who's been writing to him for weeks. Very demanding, and quite the actress in more ways than one."

"Dr Gladys Knott? Don't tell me she was tied up."

When Sarah recovered herself again from childish giggling, she turned serious. "Yep. 'I came over dizzy in the Cocktail Lounge, Officer Bradshaw'," Sarah used a mock crackly voice. "Trouble is, it only happened because her precious son – according to one technician – was getting too close to the owner of the Murder Mystery Creations lot. They're an item."

"Dr Knott and the technician?"

Sarah cackled again. "Stop! I'm going to get a stitch. No, Gladys Knott's son, Cody Spark, is going out with the boss, Myra Slade."

Janet raised a quizzical eyebrow.

"Yep, different surname. She remarried after Cody's father died. Now the second one's gone as well. Probably nagged to death!"

"Ooh, Sarah Bradshaw, I didn't have you down as having a nasty streak. I take it there wasn't anything wrong with her?"

"Blood pressure and pulse were better than mine. I gave her a dextrose tablet because she said she was prone to hypos and advised her to eat something. Cody said he'd see to it. She was much happier when I told her that the chief medical officer would make a stateroom visit on his rounds in the morning."

Janet rolled her eyes. "Poor Graham. I don't suppose I could impersonate him and pretend to be the CMO?"

Sarah laughed again; Janet's humour was awesome. She and Bernard, the male member of the nursing team who had been on board the *Coral Queen* since before Sarah joined, had hit it off from the word go, and they teased the life out of each other. Occasionally when Janet and Bernard were together, Gwen got exasperated, but other than that, all was well within the team.

"Not unless you join the Murder Mystery Creations and borrow some props! You're almost tall enough to pass as Graham's double, but you'd need one of those voice things they use in the *Mission Impossible* films to change your speech."

"I'd also need a full body corset," Janet laughed. "Graham is slightly above average BMI, although he's not in terrible shape for his age."

"Don't let him hear you say that. He's looking much younger these days. Not that he's ever told us how old he is."

"Got to be late fifties. And as for the years younger, Bernard says that's because—"

"Don't listen to Bernard. He's a mischief maker."

Janet finished her coffee. "Okay. Point taken, no gossip. Now how about that dinner?"

Sarah placed the mugs on a tray for Raggie, the medical team steward, to deal with in the morning and switched off the coffee machine. Janet turned off the light in Gwen's office and they headed towards the door, each of them dragging their medical bags behind them.

"I hope there's something good on the menu, I really need to eat," said Sarah. It was great to work with someone who liked food as much as she did. Janet had made it quite clear after joining the team she was not into health and diet regimes.

"Live and let live is my motto. I had enough of that from my ex-husband, hence the *ex*. I'm not into fat shaming; we all have our vices." Janet had somehow found the balance between self-awareness and acceptance that many struggled to come to terms with, and some never did.

Just as they reached the medical centre exit, both of their radios sprang to life.

"Code Blue, Cocktail Lounge. Repeat, Code Blue, Cocktail Lounge."

Sarah exchanged a quick glance with Janet, hoping against hope she had missed nothing serious with the troublesome Dr Gladys Knott. She pressed the button on her radio.

"Dr Plover and Nurse Bradshaw, on our way."

***

Loud music from the Cocktail Lounge greeted Sarah and Janet when they entered from the back. It was bizarre that people were clearly partying on the other side of the curtains, not realising what was happening a few metres away.

Sarah breathed a sigh of relief when she saw Gladys Knott drinking tea at a table with her son. A crewman directed them towards a man with long hair slumped back in a deckchair. She and Janet quickly assessed the situation with Janet barking a few questions at the gathering cast of characters from Murder Mystery Creations.

"I'm Doctor Plover. What happened?" she asked as she opened her medical case.

Myra was quick to answer, Sarah noticed. "He died like he was supposed to, as part of the act. Nellie Hurst – who was playing the part of a lounge singer – screamed when he fell towards her and grabbed her. I thought he was improvising, as it wasn't part of the act – he would do that sometimes. Once he had 'died', I directed a technician to close the curtains as planned. We didn't take any notice for a few minutes, but when we were ready to open the curtains to take a bow—"

A sharp-faced woman who didn't introduce herself took over the story. "I shook him to tell him to stop messing around, but he didn't move."

Sarah checked the man's pulse. "Pulse is weak, but there is one. He's tachycardic, though. Pupils are dilated and he feels hot. Is it the light in here or is he red?" Sarah asked, relieved to see Dr Graham Bentley and Bernard arrive.

"He overuses the tanning machine, always burning himself – thinks it makes him look the part," the sharp woman answered.

Janet quickly passed on what they knew to Graham, and he performed a preliminary examination. "Call down for a stretcher, Bernard. Does anyone know if he has any illnesses, allergies? Is he diabetic?"

"No allergies, but he is diabetic," the sharp woman answered again. "He takes insulin."

Sarah quickly pulled out a testing kit from her bag and used a puncture device to collect a small drop of blood onto a strip that she inserted into the monitor.

"Blood sugar's 2.1mmol."

"He's hypo, too far gone to get him to drink. Give him some buccal glucose, Sarah," Graham directed. "We'll get him down to the infirmary."

Sarah donned a pair of rubber gloves and, after the team had moved the unconscious man onto his side and checked his airway, she rubbed a glucose gel solution into the gums of his mouth.

"What's his name?" she asked.

"Dudley. Dudley Bates. I'm his wife." It surprised Sarah when the sharp-faced woman offered the last snippet of information. She appeared so cold and dismissive.

The trolley stretcher arrived, pushed by Brigitte, Sarah's French nursing colleague, and a crewman. The medical team quickly and efficiently lifted Dudley Bates onto the stretcher, and Janet put an oxygen mask over his face, the cylinder pre-attached to the trolley. His clammy state didn't bode well for his condition.

Graham recognised the seriousness. "Mrs Bates, please come with us. We'll need to ask you some questions, but first we need to stabilise your husband." As the team sped off through the rear stage doors, Sarah radioed down to Gwen to have a bed and IV ready with glucose bags. Janet was preparing an injection while the trolley was being pushed along the corridor, and she injected it into the patient's thigh as soon as they got in the lift. Bernard led Mrs Bates to the stairs as the rest crowded into the service lift.

Once they arrived on deck two where the medical centre and infirmary were situated, Gwen met them, and she and Brigitte took the stretcher and raced towards the infirmary with Graham walking ahead to be ready to treat the still unconscious Dudley Bates. Janet and Sarah were slower because they still had to drag their on-call bags behind them.

Janet whispered what Sarah was thinking. "I never would have believed she was his wife. She seemed so detached."

"Me neither. I heard that he and Myra had had an affair, though. Maybe they haven't made up."

"That would explain it. Good job your friend Rachel wasn't there, or I'd start to believe the rumours," Janet cackled.

"She was there," groaned Sarah. "Lady Marjorie – our eccentric elderly friend – is treating her to the murder mystery bash."

"I thought you said she worked for CID?"

"She does, but Marjorie can be determined. Rachel's not happy about it, but she adores the old woman." Sarah shrugged.

"Let's be thankful this is a plain and simple hypo, then."

There was no more time to chat, as it was all hands on deck when they got Dudley onto a bed. His condition hadn't improved, despite buccal and intramuscular glucose. Janet inserted an IV line using the needle Gwen had prepared and ran a dextrose solution through full pelt.

Graham placed a stethoscope over the man's heart. "He's still not improving. I don't understand it. Sarah. Can you find where Bernard's put his wife and ask if he's taken anything else this evening."

"You mean drugs?" Sarah quizzed.

Graham nodded. "You know what these theatrical types can be like; his pupils are dilated when they shouldn't be. He could be a user for all we know. His nostrils show signs of cocaine use."

Sarah knew how much Graham hated drug abuse, but she had no idea why. He was usually tolerant and patient with all manner of human frailty, but on this subject, he verged on judgemental. She noticed Gwen giving a quick squeeze to the senior medical officer's forearm, unseen by anyone else.

So the rumours are true. At least that was something to be happy about. Graham and Gwen both deserved some good fortune. Graham was a widower who took to the seas to escape memories of his loving wife, vowing never to marry again. And poor Gwen had been involved in an affair with another CMO on her previous ship after he convinced her he was in a loveless marriage, but the reality was he had just been after a bit on the side as Bernard, her incorrigible Filipino colleague, put it.

Sarah found Bernard pouring Mrs Bates a cup of coffee. Raggie, their ever-reliable medical team steward, had obviously heard there was a crisis and as always had ordered drinks from the kitchen. Bernard's raised eyebrow told Sarah he was not getting very far with the unwavering Mrs Bates. The woman sat upright in a waiting room chair, mousy brown hair permed tightly to her head. She was around forty, Sarah guessed, with thin lips and a large mole covering the left side of her neck. Although she was wearing plentiful makeup and concealer, the mark stood out. Her bright red gel nails sat in her lap and she wore an old-fashioned maroon evening gown Sarah assumed was for her role in the show.

"Mrs Bates, I'm Sarah Bradshaw. Dr Bentley has asked me to—"

The emergency bell sounding from the infirmary interrupted Sarah's words. Raggie immediately appeared and sat with Mrs Bates while Sarah and Bernard raced to attend.

Chapter 5

The buffet was quiet when Rachel arrived, with just a few passengers milling around at the early hour of 7.45am. She had already run ten laps of the track on deck sixteen and spent forty minutes in the gym, having awoken early with the events of the previous evening whizzing round in her head. How she wished Marjorie hadn't booked them onto a murder mystery event because, real or not, her curiosity had been awakened and she was determined to get to the bottom of the supposed murder of the disagreeable Marvin Black, aka Dudley Bates.

She helped herself to a bowl of muesli, adding fresh fruit salad and plain yoghurt to the top. Passing the pastry stand, she was drawn by the aroma of freshly baked croissants, so she grabbed a plate and took one, along with butter and apricot jam. Sarah hadn't arrived yet, so she found a table on the starboard side of the ship and plonked her tray down with a sigh.

As she stared out on the North Sea, her thoughts turned once again to the murder scene. She had been watching closely and still couldn't work out who had poisoned Marvin Black. For it was poison – of that she was certain. She was annoyed at not having been able to access the rerun on the stateroom TV channel when she got back to her room the night before.

She took a large spoonful of muesli and chastised herself as she munched. "You need to get a grip, Prince. You're supposed to be on holiday."

"Precisely," came a welcome voice approaching from behind. Rachel turned around to see Sarah carrying a tray laden with a large fry up.

"Sarah! Was I talking to myself? That's worrying." Feeling embarrassed about how seriously she was taking the mock murder, Rachel stood and hugged her friend – after allowing Sarah to put the tray down on the table. "It's so good to see you."

"And you. Where's Marjorie? I thought she was joining us."

"When I called her after my workout, she said she would have breakfast in her room. She's tired; it was rather a late night in the end. It might have more to do with the fact she's not a huge fan of the buffet, though."

Sarah laughed before tucking into her breakfast. "I'm starving," she explained to an amused Rachel. "Why were you talking to yourself, anyway? Is something on your mind?"

"Not really. It's this silly murder mystery Marjorie roped me into. It surprised me how good the performance was, so realistic, but don't tell Marjorie I said that. I've been trying to work out who poisoned Marvin Black ever since." She giggled at how ludicrous she must sound.

Sarah stopped eating for a moment and her hazel eyes locked with Rachel's.

"I'm assuming you mean the murder victim played by Dudley Bates. What makes you think it was poison?"

"I've read enough Agatha Christie to acquaint myself with the symptoms of common poisoning. Not to mention, I've been studying a book on toxins and poison."

Sarah rolled her eyes. "Hopefully you've brought along something a little more along the lines of a romcom for your holiday."

Rachel polished off her breakfast, smirking. "Maybe," she teased. "Anyway, the poison in question was Deadly Nightshade, if I'm not mistaken."

Sarah's head shot up and there was a clatter as she dropped her knife and fork onto her plate. "OMG! You could be right. I need to get down to the medical centre." Sarah sprang up and raced out of the buffet, speaking hurriedly into her radio, but she wasn't fast enough to escape Rachel, courtesy of the heavy case she dragged behind her.

"Sarah! Wait for me. What's going on?"

Sarah waited by the lift, shaking her head, warning Rachel not to speak as a few passengers assembled nearby. Ever the professional cruise ship officer, she smiled at the guests after getting in the lift, asking polite questions about whether they were enjoying their holiday.

Once the passengers exited, Rachel put hands on hips, waiting for a response.

"I'm under strict instructions not to talk about this, so you're going to have to be patient for once in your life." Sarah chewed her bottom lip, a telltale warning sign of deep worry as they descended the next few floors in silence. The lift stopped on deck two and the automated announcement confirmed they had reached their destination. Rachel sighed heavily, accepting it was no use trying to get Sarah to say anything else just now. Once her friend's mind was made up, there was no shifting her. However, Rachel wasn't leaving until she knew what was going on. Except deep down, she already knew her worst fears about the previous evening were about to be confirmed.

Rachel trailed Sarah, who was still motoring as fast as her case would allow her, into the senior nurse Gwen Sumner's office. Dr Bentley, Gwen, Bernard and Brigitte – all people Rachel had got to know over the past few years – were sitting in armchairs around a large coffee table on the informal side of the room. Dr Bentley beamed at her just as another woman burst into the office.

"What's going on?" the newcomer asked. She was a bit shorter than Rachel's five foot ten inches, with large brown eyes and wavy red hair just below her shoulders. A nose full of freckles gave her a young appearance.

"We're just about to find out. Sarah has something urgent she wants to discuss. I expect this has something to do with you, Rachel?" Dr Bentley said.

"I think so, although Sarah hasn't told me why she's turned into Road Runner yet."

The new arrival, who Rachel assumed was the latest baby doc, as the junior on board ship was referred to, guffawed. "The woman I've heard so much about. I wasn't sure she existed; I was convinced she was a newbie windup."

"Oh, she exists all right," Bernard butted in with a mischievous grin slapped on his face. "And by the look on Sarah's face, there's been another murder."

"Don't sound so gleeful about it, Bernard. If there has been, it's no laughing matter," reprimanded Gwen. "Why don't we all sit down and let Sarah speak? Rachel, this is Dr Janet Plover, our new doctor. Janet, this is Rachel Jacobi-Prince. Now let's have a bit of order. And stop bickering, you two." Gwen turned her attention to Bernard and Brigitte. The French nurse was obviously not as enamoured as her male colleague about the prospect of foul play.

Having brought the room to order, Gwen handed coffees and teas around.

"I take it someone has died?" Rachel quizzed.

Dr Bentley looked grim. "One of the actors from the Murder Mystery Creations took ill last night after the show. It appeared he went into hypoglycaemic shock – a rare condition – but I take it from Sarah, she now believes otherwise."

All heads turned towards Sarah, who flushed under the spotlight. "It was Rachel who put me onto it. I think someone poisoned him during the performance."

Gasps filled the room and Bernard nudged Brigitte, mouthing, 'Told you'.

"Please enlighten us, Sarah." Dr Bentley shot an impatient glare at Bernard. "What makes you think it was poison?"

"Well, Rachel is one of the guests attending the 'Murder on Deck' event, along with Lady Marjorie Snellthorpe. They were there at the time the fictional character died."

"Where is dear Lady Snellthorpe?" asked Bernard.

"She was tired after travelling yesterday and our rather late night," Rachel replied quickly, aware that the chief medical officer wanted to move things along.

Sarah nodded before continuing. "While we were having breakfast, Rachel said she had concluded that the cause of death was Deadly Nightshade."

Dr Plover's jaw dropped as she slapped her head. "Atropa belladonna, or atropine in the form we medics use."

"Of course!" cried Dr Bentley. "That would explain the redness and the heat along with the dilated pupils. His wife said he was always like that after a show. What with that and the makeup, plus the fact he was a diabetic with low blood sugar, foul play didn't occur to me. Tell me what signs you observed, Rachel."

Rachel described how Marvin-cum-Dudley had appeared to convulse, grabbing hold of the actress, Nellie Hurst, before complaining of the heat and dropping the glass of champagne he was drinking from.

"He then slumped onto the floor. Everyone assumed it was just an impressive performance. It almost convinced me."

"Why do you say almost?" asked Gwen.

It was Rachel's turn to feel all eyes upon her. "It seemed so real. I know it's meant to, but afterwards, I heard some scuffling about behind the curtains, and the two women we were sitting with remarked on how the cast usually take a bow at the end of the show."

"If this is murder – and, on reflection, I'm considering it a real possibility – did you see who and how?" Dr Bentley asked.

"I think the how would be the glass of champagne, but as for the who, that's where the actors were adept at ensuring they were all suspects for us to ponder."

"So this could be the perfect murder carried out on stage where everyone sees something, but no-one sees anything." Gwen got up from her seat. "I'd better call

Chief Waverley. He'll want to talk to you, Rachel, but it might be better if we tell him first."

"That's fine with me. I need to catch Marjorie anyway and tell her what's happened. She may have noticed something. Is it too much to hope they've cancelled the rest of the nights?"

"You mean you're not enjoying solving crime on your holiday?" quipped Bernard, who couldn't help himself.

The comment drew a scowl from Gwen. "To work, the rest of you. Graham and I have calls to make."

The nurses obediently left the office with Rachel, Janet Plover following and muttering.

"I really thought your reputation was a windup," she said to Rachel once they were out in the corridor.

"Sorry. I'm real, and me being a murder magnet is unfortunately true."

"My money's on natural causes," the doctor replied.

"I'd better contact a pathologist and ask them to look for atropine. I have to say, this was almost the perfect murder," Rachel heard Graham say as he too left Gwen's office. Rachel wasn't sure whether the news would thrill or horrify Marjorie.

I'm about to find out, she thought five minutes later, knocking on her elderly friend's stateroom door.

Chapter 6

Half an hour after leaving the medical centre, Rachel had told Marjorie the complete story, along with the possibility that someone had committed a murder right under their noses.

"I should have listened to you; you were right last night when you said something was going on behind the curtains. And it wasn't just a technical glitch."

Rachel grimaced as she poured herself and Marjorie fresh cups of tea. "It appears not. There was something going on, but then Dudley Bates was diabetic, so Dr Bentley's initial diagnosis could still be the right one. He's ringing a coroner and pathologist on land to ask them to do toxicology and chromatography to look for the poison."

"Deadly Nightshade is also known as belladonna or atropine, isn't it?" Marjorie quizzed. "I watched a documentary on naturally occurring poisons recently."

"Yes, to all the above."

"And do they really believe it was murder?"

"It's a strong possibility, and Dr Bentley agrees the symptoms fit in retrospect. If it was foul play, according to Gwen, it was almost the perfect murder."

"She's right there. I seem to remember it's practically undetectable at post-mortem, unless one actively seeks it out."

"I heard that too."

"Of course, this means they will cancel the 'Murder on Deck' event. I'm sorry, Rachel, I thought it would be fun, and now we have another real murder to solve. We can't leave it to you know who."

Marjorie had little trust in the security chief's ability to solve murders and tended to be disparaging to him whenever the opportunity arose. Unfortunately, Jack Waverley's past blunders had given Rachel's friend enough ammunition to be unrelenting. Waverley, on the other hand, had a tendency to get flustered around Marjorie, causing him to go off into nervous coughing bouts and jump to clumsy conclusions.

Rachel got on well with him, except when he pulled rank and warned her away from investigating. She considered him a friend, but there was tension in their relationship, as there were times he welcomed her help and others when he forbade it. She hoped he'd be in an amenable frame of mind when it was their turn to be interviewed and suspected it wouldn't be too long until she found out.

"The medical team believe the show's continuing."

Marjorie fiddled with the TV remote, throwing it down in disgust. "Where's Mario? I can't find the blasted channel."

Mario, the butler for the suites Marjorie and Rachel occupied, was usually to hand whenever they needed him, so much so that Rachel often wondered if he had a sixth sense. As if on cue, he knocked and entered.

"Is there anything I can get you, ladies?"

"Can you get this TV to work? I can't find the special channel supposedly available for guests of the murder mystery event."

Rachel noticed a flicker of an upturned lip on the butler's face as he took the remote.

"Let me try, Lady Snellthorpe."

"I don't think it's working," offered Rachel. "I tried earlier in my room. Perhaps it's not streaming yet."

After several failed attempts, Mario sighed. "I'll find out for you what's happening."

"Don't worry for now, Mario, but when you do contact someone, could you also ask what time the event is taking place this evening?" Marjorie was subtle enough not to mention there may have been a real-life murder in front of Mario.

"Of course, ma'am. Is there anything else?"

"No, thank you," Rachel answered. "It's time for Lady Marjorie's constitutional."

"My what? Oh yes, of course, dear. I need to take some daily exercise."

A bemused Mario left them in peace.

"What was that about my constitutional?"

"I think it's time we walked around the ship as guests of 'Murder on Deck' to see whether we can extract any information from anyone in the cast. If we can track them down, that is."

"Oh, good idea. We'll behave as if we don't realise anything is amiss and pretend to be investigating the death of Marvin Black. It's going to seem strange enquiring about a pretend death which has turned out to be an actual death. Talk about macabre. Who would conceive of such a thing?"

"Someone who's clever, and also brazen," replied Rachel. "This person will be under the illusion they have got away with murder. We're looking for someone devious and heartless enough to kill a man in front of their colleagues and a fairly large audience without a shred of fear. I could almost imagine this wasn't the first time they have killed."

"Either that, or they took ideas from Agatha Christie and put them into a real-life murder. Any ideas as to who it might be?"

"Assuming it is murder and not natural causes, it could be any one of the cast. We know the dead man had an affair with Myra Slade and I bet his wife knew about it, so she goes top of the list."

"Then there's Myra herself."

"Yep, or her boyfriend. We don't know whether she had the affair with the dead man while she was going out with him. We need to check."

"I suppose any one of the others could also carry a grudge for reasons we're not aware of yet, but you're right, Rachel. We start with Don's wife."

"Dudley."

"His wife's called Dudley?"

"No, he was Dudley, remember? His wife's Leanne; she was acting as the duchess's sister, Dora Michaels."

"How do you remember all this? Don't tell me, the programme!"

Rachel laughed before continuing. "We need to be circumspect. Remember, we don't know for sure yet there was a real murder, or that Deadly Nightshade was the poison used."

"Goodie! This is going to be even more fun than I imagined," chuckled Marjorie, clearly warming to the task in hand. "Even if it wasn't an actual murder, I still want us to be the first to crack the case, as they say."

"Don't let Waverley hear you say that."

"Pah! Who's bothered about him? He'll need our help, he always does."

Rachel half-grinned at her friend. *At least someone's enjoying the turn of events.*

Chapter 7

Jack Waverley was deliberating the quandary he was in. He had more or less decided not to formally interview members of the Murder Mystery Creations cast. It made sense to allow the murderer to think they had got away with it and for everyone to believe – as first thought – that Dudley Bates had died from hypoglycaemia.

Nevertheless, he was agitated. Would he be comfortable with not being able to press for answers? Leaving the investigating to Rachel Jacobi-Prince would not be without its problems, the main one being that Queen Cruises did not employ her and he might be putting her and Lady Snellthorpe at risk. On the other hand, she had proved useful to him in the past and they had successfully solved murders committed on board.

He stared at the computer in front of him. Background checks on the Creations cast members should arrive soon, but he was impatient to do something.

A knock at his office door pulled him from his maudlin thoughts. He waved a hand to indicate to Jason Goodridge, a member of his security team, to enter.

"Goodridge, good afternoon. I take it you've heard about the Bates fellow's death?"

"Yes, sir. It was in the night report. Natural causes according to Dr Bentley."

Waverley coughed. "That was the initial conclusion; it now seems, erm… we are now treating the death as suspicious. Coffee?"

"Yes please, sir. Suspicious as in murder or suicide?"

"The former, I'm afraid. Take a seat and I'll fill you in. You've obviously not spoken to Sarah yet today."

"No, sir. The night shift was busy – a few drunken brawls and a theft. I got a few hours' shuteye before coming back on duty."

"Quite. I read your report on the theft. You suspect a passenger. We must tread carefully on that one."

"Yes. The steward says he saw a passenger leaving the wrong room. He was cleaning the bathroom at the time. When he called out to the woman, she ignored him and gave him the slip. I pulled CCTV footage. The woman in question is a Mrs Brewer from the eighth floor. I'm going to speak to her in a little while and see what she has to say after I present her with the evidence."

"Right. Well, I'll leave that one to you. Let me know if you need me, won't you?"

"Yes, sir."

Waverley indicated for Jason to take a seat in the comfortable chairs positioned in the open area of his office. He handed him the coffee, poured from his own percolator, and took another chair.

"Now. About the death of Mr Dudley Bates. As you know, he was male, aged forty-seven, married to Leanne Bates who's on board. They have no children. According to his medical records, he was a diabetic on insulin. His wife wasn't overly helpful according to Graham Bentley, but she believes he took insulin before last night's performance and may have skipped dinner for reasons unknown. I've checked his background, and it revealed he'd had some arrests for drugs offences – using rather than dealing – the last one a year ago."

"Hard drugs?"

"Mostly marijuana, but some cocaine use. Dr Bentley wondered if he had taken cocaine last night, and had asked the pathologist to check on that prior to what we learned this morning via…"

"Rachel Jacobi-Prince, I suspect?"

Waverley coughed; Rachel had a reputation on board the ship for being a murder magnet. Jason had a lot of respect for her, which was just as well when she was his fiancée's best friend.

"Indeed, you guessed right. It seems she and Lady Marjorie are guests at the Murder Mystery Creations' maiden event. The first act was last night and Rachel suspected the actor who died – who was playing a character called Marvin Black, the victim of the fictional murder – was poisoned with Deadly Nightshade, or atropine as it is more commonly called by the medics. Quite by chance, she was discussing the fictional murder with Sarah over breakfast when Sarah realised that poison really could have caused Mr Bates's death."

Jason rubbed his hand through his hair. "And did it?"

"We should know very soon, but the good doctor now believes it's a more realistic cause of death than hypoglycaemia or low blood sugar."

"I see. You said the wife was unhelpful. Is she a suspect?"

"She and the rest of the cast. It had to be someone familiar with the script who was on the stage at the time of the pretend-cum-actual death. This gives us six suspects. Once we have confirmation of cause of death, we will know more."

The telephone on Waverley's desk rang. He stood and picked up the receiver. "Hello, Chief of Security, Jack Waverley, speaking. Yes… And you're sure? Right. Thank you." He put the receiver down and turned to Jason. With a heavy sigh, he said, "Confirmed atropine poisoning. We do have a murder on our hands."

Jason drank back his coffee as Waverley joined him again. "Do you want me to start questioning the cast?"

"Erm… Yes and no. It's a bit convoluted, but the way they conduct the murder mystery event allows passengers to question the actors at any time whenever they see them. They quiz them and try to work out who killed the victim – in this case, Marvin Black, a washed-up pop star. I thought it might be pertinent to allow Rachel to do some poking around for now. Myra Slade, the CEO, doesn't want passengers knowing about the untimely death anyway, and the cast all seem keen to continue with the show. We ran it past events management, and it made and still makes sense to allow the show to go on."

"Even now we know it is murder?"

"Yes, because whoever did this thinks they've got away with it, which gives us the element of surprise. Let's face it, what are the chances of having Rachel, a friend of a nurse on board and a CID detective, as a guest of the event? That piece of luck gives us the upper hand."

"I'm surprised Rachel wanted to take part in a murder mystery. Doesn't she get enough of that on land?" Jason asked.

"According to Sarah, it wasn't her choice."

"Ah. The formidable Lady Marjorie?"

"Just so. Anyway, for now, I'm going to speak with Rachel, and if she's willing, we'll let her run with it, but we can still quiz the cast as a matter of routine because there's been a sudden death on board. I suggest we take three each, and let's try to keep the actual cause of death between ourselves for now. We don't want any loose talk getting back to the Murder Mystery Creations employees or we'll lose the element of surprise."

"Yes, sir. I won't tell anyone, then. When are you going to meet up with Rachel? And I expect Lady Marjorie won't be kept out of this."

"Sarah says they'll most likely be in Creams this afternoon. I'll catch them then. I won't arrange a follow-up, but you'll know where they will be later tonight, I presume?"

"They often meet Sarah in the Jazz Bar after she finishes evening surgery. I guess they'll meet her after the second act tonight."

"Good. If Rachel doesn't want to get involved, I'll let you know, but experience tells me she won't pass up the opportunity. I wish Lady Marjorie wasn't on board, but Rachel will keep her safe. You can catch up with them later. I'm still waiting for background checks on our six suspects.

"We need to consider means and motive. They all had an opportunity. You take the wife of the deceased, Leanne Bates; see what you think of her. I'll take Myra Slade, the boss. She's a friend of Tatum's, so we'll need to make sure she doesn't get a whiff of this. I'd better take the old dear – she's a retired medic, Graham tells me. You can take her son, Cody Spark; he's a vet and not a regular. I can't see him being involved."

"Why's that?"

"I don't think he knows the cast; he's only here because of his relationship with Ms Slade. So is his mother, for that matter. You can also take Demos Benedict, thirty-nine-year-old actor. That leaves me with Nellie Hurst, a sixty-two-year-old actress.

"Actually, the more I think about this, the more I'm convinced it has to be the wife. She's top of the list and most likely thinks she's scored a home run."

Jason looked up from where he had been taking notes. "Would you like to question her yourself, then, sir?"

"No. Let her believe it's just routine enquiries. She'll be more at ease with you than with me."

"Good point. Okay, I'll wrap up the theft case, and then track down the three on my list. I'll nip into the main security office to see if the backgrounds are back before speaking to them."

Waverley paused, wondering again if he was approaching the case in the right way. Particularly as he now knew rather than suspected the death was murder.

"Is there something else, sir?" Jason asked, glancing at him.

Realising he was staring into space, Waverley stood. "Nothing else. Carry on, Goodridge. Meet me here this evening before you meet with Rachel, unless either of us comes up with anything significant in the meantime."

"Right, sir." Jason rose and headed towards the door.

"Goodridge?"

"Yes, sir?"

Waverley pondered whether to share his doubts with Jason. He trusted him; the man was loyal to a fault.

"Never mind. See you later."

"Right, sir."

Waverley returned to his desk, staring at the screen. He picked up the phone and called Graham Bentley, the chief medical officer. Graham would understand his conundrum and was the same rank.

Chapter 8

Rachel and Marjorie had checked almost all the busiest areas from decks three to six, but hadn't caught sight of anyone from the Creations group.

"This is frustrating," remarked Marjorie. "On a ship this size, we could walk around for days and still not see any of them."

"I wonder if they usually give out clues as to where they'll be after the performance. Remember, they didn't get the chance to close properly last night."

"I expect you're right. I don't know about you, but I'm rather peckish. Why don't we have lunch and resume our search afterwards?"

Rachel took Marjorie's arm. "Agreed. Where to?"

"The Coral Restaurant, of course." Marjorie liked to eat in style in the premier restaurant at set dining times. As they had eaten in the Cocktail Lounge the previous evening, they hadn't yet been to the Coral Restaurant since boarding.

"As long as you don't expect me to eat a three course meal before a five course meal tonight."

"You could go to the buffet if you'd prefer and I'll meet you later. Did you arrange to meet up with Sarah again?"

"No. It all went a bit awry this morning. I expect we'll catch her this afternoon in Creams; she'll know where to find us. I'm happy to join you in the restaurant for lunch."

The restaurant was packed with passengers enjoying the wealth of food available on their sea day. The next few days, the ship would dock in ports along the Norwegian coastline, so Rachel didn't mind succumbing to the temptation of table service for one lunch.

Marjorie enjoyed the pampering from the senior waiter and his assistant along with the bustle of the restaurant, while Rachel had to force herself to relax. Used to eating on the go, she wasn't a fan of sitting around waiting to be served at the best of times. Now it was considerably worse because she wanted to get on with a murder investigation – real or fake.

"I can see, you know," Marjorie chuckled.

"See what?"

"You're fidgeting." Marjorie's eyes twinkled in the light from the chandeliers hanging from the marble effect laminated ceiling.

"Sorry."

Their table waiter, who had introduced himself as Basil, appeared to clear away their bowls. "Would you like coffee, ladies?"

Usually, Rachel would not pass up the opportunity of coffee, but this time, thankfully, even Marjorie decided it was time to move.

"No thank you, Basil. Time for some exercise after the wonderful food."

Basil pulled back Marjorie's chair to ease her exit, and his assistant appeared behind Rachel to do the same for her. The efficiency of the staff always impressed her. Marjorie took Rachel's arm, and they vacated the busy restaurant.

"Shall we try the Lido Deck?" Rachel asked.

"Yes. It's a lovely day, perhaps we'll find some Creations." Marjorie laughed at her own joke. "And if not, we can have that coffee in the fresh air."

"Now you're talking," agreed Rachel.

As soon as they arrived on the Lido Deck, Rachel spotted one of the actors, the Carlos lookalike. She sighed heavily at the reminder of how much she missed her husband, but pulled herself out of the ever-threatening melancholy. Nudging Marjorie, she pointed her head in the direction of the burger bar where Demos Benedict stood in a queue.

"Good. That's one man I would like to speak to. Isn't he the one who has a rather loose tongue?"

"Judging by what Enid said yesterday, I'd say you're right. He's also disgruntled, from what they implied."

"And a ladies' man. Time to use your charm, Rachel."

"I don't believe you at times, Marjorie Snellthorpe. I refuse to flirt with him, if that's what you're suggesting." Rachel hoped, rather than believed this to be true.

"He reminds me of someone, you know," said Marjorie, obviously seeing Rachel flush as understanding crossed her face. "Oh, I see now: our Carlos. I think we'd better leave me to handle Mr – what's his surname again?"

"Benedict," said Rachel. "And – for your information – just because there's a minute resemblance to Carlos doesn't mean I would fall for his charms."

"Of course not, dear. Shall we go and talk to him, then?"

"Let him get his lunch first. Too many people around him. Come on, we'll find a table and order coffee. I'm parched."

They sat at a table overlooking the sea, but with an excellent view of passengers going to and from the grill bar. They had ordered coffee from a passing drinks waiter, and still Demos hadn't been served. The queue had lengthened, mainly because of the three people in front of Demos requesting enormous amounts of freshly cooked burgers and sausages.

When their coffees arrived, Rachel noted familiar faces off to their right. "Don't turn around, but we're not the only ones waiting for Demos."

Rachel might have known as soon as she said don't turn around that Marjorie would do just that. "Ah, his mother and daughter fan club."

Rachel grinned. Enid and Kate were drinking tea at a table well positioned to arrest Demos in his tracks as soon as he was served and headed their way. Enid's hair floated in the breeze. She was dressed casually in white cropped trousers, a yellow t-shirt and a white cotton jacket. Kate's long fair hair was tied back in a ponytail. She wore thick makeup and bright pink lipstick, denim shorts and a revealing sky blue vest. Lettuce from a burger roll fell onto her lap, the green standing out against the blue as she hunched over, munching into the roll and a plate of cooked chips.

"We may not get a look in here. Those two haven't taken their eyes off the target."

Marjorie grinned back at Rachel, sipping her coffee. "Enid looks amazing, doesn't she?"

"I feel sorry for Kate. She's obviously besotted with Demos, but with her mother around, I don't think she stands a chance."

"I expect her mother's the one with the money, too. I'm pretty sure that's where his sights truly lie."

Rachel noticed a flirtatious exchange of smiles between Demos and Enid, who quickly checked to see if her daughter had noticed.

"They both fancy him, but I suspect Enid won't do anything to hurt her daughter. They seem close."

"We might need them to prompt him to open up. Do you think we should enlist their help or pretend it's the fictional murder we're interested in?"

Rachel laughed. "I was just thinking the same thing. Enid is the more likely person to be able to control her emotions. And he's shared stuff with her before. I don't think Kate would be capable of being objective. We'll see how things go."

They finished their coffee and watched as Demos finally got served and joined the two women. Soon giggling and flirtatious laughter filled the air.

"Come on, Marjorie. We'll think about speaking to Enid later. I've just spotted someone else we can tackle."

Chapter 9

Cody Spark was leaning against a ship's rail, staring out to sea, when Rachel and Marjorie joined him.

"Hello. Is it a good time to talk?" Rachel kicked off.

He jumped back. "Pardon?"

"About the murder scene last night," explained Rachel. "We're 'Murder on Deck' guests. I'm Rachel and this is my good friend, Marjorie."

Cody stood a few inches shorter than Rachel, but a good five inches taller than Marjorie, who was slight. Thick lenses inside silver-rimmed spectacles caused his green eyes to seem huge as he looked at them. He was slightly overweight with a paunch and had dark brown hair with greying sideburns.

"Oh yes. Of course. I was miles away. I'm not sure I will be of any great help, though, as I don't work for the Murder Mystery Creations."

"But you were on stage last night. I'm sure I saw you. You were the waiter, if I'm not mistaken?" Marjorie intervened.

Cody seemed uncomfortable, hopping from one foot to the other and fiddling with his glasses. "Erm. Yes. I'm helping out just this once. But my role is minor. The other actors will be better placed to answer questions."

"Well, we can't ask Marvin Black, as he's dead, isn't he?" Marjorie pressed.

"What? How did you know?" Cody's paling face worried Rachel, who thought he might collapse any moment.

"We were at the show. He was the rock star who died. It seemed to me to be poison. Am I right?"

Cody recovered. "I don't think I can tell you that," he mumbled. "I can only answer questions about my role, and as I said, it was fairly minor."

Rachel wanted to push him, but sensed him closing down. "You say you don't work for the Creations group. What do you do when you're not cruising?"

Visibly relaxing, Cody answered, "I'm a vet."

"Better with animals than people, then," Marjorie smiled.

Cody stopped hopping and brushed back his hair. "Something like that. This isn't my thing, but my girlfriend persuaded my mother to take part. Mother was keen, as she's never been on a cruise, but wouldn't do it unless I took a part too, so I agreed."

"I see. Is your mother the duchess, Christine Bloom?" Rachel glanced at her programme.

"Yes, she is acting as the duchess. Her actual name is Gladys. Gladys Knott. Mother used to do amateur dramatics in her spare time. This is much more her than me. As you said, Marjorie, I'm better with animals."

"But good with names," Marjorie smiled again, encouraging the shy man.

"Yes, I'm one of those lucky – or unlucky – people with a photographic memory."

"So you'll be able to tell us exactly where everyone was at the time of the murder?" Rachel suggested.

"I'm only allowed to tell you certain things, and only if you ask the right questions."

Rachel was pleased Cody was relaxing and obviously felt at ease with Marjorie. *Perhaps because she is older, and he dotes on his mother*, she mused.

"Okay," Marjorie said, "did you give Marvin Black the drink that killed him?"

Cody's right eye twitched. "I served him and everyone else in the room champagne, but I don't know what killed him. In fact, now you mention it, I didn't give him the champagne. Mother – sorry, the duchess – asked me to put the tray on a nearby table. I think he must have helped himself."

Rachel remembered the tray being placed on a round table and the guests in the scene helping themselves. She didn't remember Marvin Black taking a drink, but assumed he must have done.

"From my recollection," said Marjorie, "the man cursed that the others had left no drinks for him and snatched one from the makeshift bar on set."

"I don't know," said Cody, sticking to his script. "I left the tray and went to get Mother – sorry – the duchess a brandy."

Rachel was kicking herself. Why couldn't she remember what happened? "Blast. That must have been when the crowd next to us started postulating what was going to happen next," she muttered out loud.

Marjorie chuckled. "Are you having a private conversation with yourself, Rachel?"

"Sorry. I was wondering why I couldn't remember where everyone was at the time drinks were served. Now I know."

"I have nothing else I can tell you, ladies. Sorry," said Cody.

"Just one more thing," Marjorie said, clearly enjoying herself. "Are you in a relationship with that lounge singer?"

"I don't know what you're talking about," Cody replied, clearly sticking to his lines.

"Thank you, Todd," said Rachel, smiling. "You've been most unhelpful."

He laughed for the first time. "Oh good. I must be getting into it. My proper name's Cody, by the way. Cody Spark."

"Didn't you say your mother's surname was Knott?" quizzed Marjorie.

"Yes, it's complicated. Mother married again after my father died and took the name Bright, but my stepfather died a couple of years ago. Now she's gone back to using her maiden name. She was a doctor and practised under her maiden name all her working life."

"A doctor. How interesting. Was she a GP?" Marjorie asked.

"No. Mother was a consultant neurologist. She wanted me to be a doctor, but animals are my thing. I find people d-difficult," he stuttered.

"How did you meet Myra?" Marjorie quizzed. Rachel nudged her friend. They weren't supposed to know who his girlfriend was.

"M-Myra and I met when sh-she b-brought her c-c-c-c-at into surgery." The more pronounced stutter told Rachel he had picked up on Marjorie's mistake.

"Marjorie Snellthorpe, I've always said you have a sixth sense. Is Myra Slade your girlfriend?" Rachel hoped her act would work.

It did. Cody grinned. "Yes. I wondered how you knew." He looked at Marjorie.

"Oh, I'm a sucker for love," she took her cue. "I believe you and she exchanged a brief handhold before the performance. At my age, you have nothing better to do than revel in other people's happiness."

"Mother's the same. She notices every exchange between me and Myra. I try not to make it too obvious, though. I don't want her to feel left out. Speaking of my mother, I promised to meet her in the library. Would you excuse me, please?"

"That was enlightening, wasn't it?" remarked Marjorie when he left.

"Only in so far as he's not the one we're going to get any gossip from. He's incapable. Sarah says he's henpecked, and after the revelation of his mother noticing everything about his relationship, we can gather she's clearly let him know she feels left out."

"Adores his mother, though. That must be nice..." Marjorie's voice trailed off as she stared wistfully out to sea.

"I don't believe for one minute you'd like Jeremy to be glued to you."

"Actually, you're right. And I know he loves me in his own way. I wonder sometimes whether it's my fault he doesn't show his emotions."

"As you say, he loves you. Isn't that more important than faffing around with hugs and kisses? Anyway, I'm not sure Gladys Knott wants her son to have any sort of relationship. She's one of those 'no-one will ever be good enough for my son' types. If it had been Myra who died, I'd believe she had something to do with it."

"We need to speak with her at some point, though. We're not getting very far, are we?"

"We're only just starting." Rachel looked at her watch. "It's 3pm. Shall we see if Sarah's in Creams?"

Chapter 10

As Rachel headed with Marjorie towards the entrance of their favourite patisserie, she noticed the large frame of the chief of security, Jack Waverley, hanging around outside. He coughed as they approached, a habit he had when delivering sensitive information, or when embarrassed, as he must be now.

"Rachel Jacobi-Prince, Lady Marjorie. How nice to see you."

Marjorie huffed, "Chief." She proffered her hand, which he took and shook politely.

"Chief Waverley. Good to see you too. Were you heading in the same direction as us?"

"I wouldn't want to intrude, but I thought I might find you both here." He gave a sheepish glance towards Marjorie, who could sometimes be offhand, verging on rude, to him.

"Oh, do join us. I expect you want to discuss yesterday evening. We were hoping Sarah would be here." Rachel looked inside the patisserie.

"She's on her way up. I radioed her when I saw you."

Marjorie had clearly had enough of the chitchat. "Well, shall we stand here all afternoon or find a table?"

Rachel took her arm and tapped it soothingly. "Do you want to find out what's going on or not?" she whispered.

Marjorie got the message and grinned. "Yes, do join us, Chief." Rachel knew, deep down, Marjorie was fond of Jack Waverley, but she could never quite forgive him for having had her followed on the cruise where they'd first met. He'd done it for her safety, but Marjorie had been worried sick about being followed, and it turned out to be a security guard. She'd dismissed the fact she was also being followed by Rachel's own beloved Carlos, and by a hitman, and held Waverley responsible for all her suffering.

A waiter appeared within a nanosecond of the chief entering the patisserie. "Good afternoon, sir. What can we do for you?"

"Relax, man." He tapped the waiter on the arm. "I'm here for afternoon tea with some old friends. Could you find us a table away from prying eyes?"

"Right away, sir. Come this way." They followed the flustered waiter to the rear of Creams where they were shown to the table they always used, behind a pillar and set apart from the rest.

"Officer Bradshaw will be joining us. Point her in the right direction, will you?"

"Yes, sir. You can count on me, sir."

After he'd gone, Marjorie chuckled. "He's new here, isn't he? Such reverence, Chief. Don't let it go to your head."

Waverley coughed. "A little respect doesn't do any harm now and then."

"Quite," said Marjorie. "But respect and obeisance are quite different."

"I erm…"

"Ignore her, Chief. She's winding you up." Rachel shot Marjorie a disapproving frown. "Look, here's Sarah."

Sarah appeared in fresh whites and her face shone as she hugged Rachel again. "Sorry about this morning." She turned and hugged Marjorie, kissing her on the cheek before taking a seat. "Have you ordered? I'm starving."

"You're always starving, young lady," Marjorie rebuked while chuckling at the same time. Sarah's bubbly presence relaxed any tension that might have heightened between Waverley and Marjorie.

Rachel grinned. "We were waiting for you. Here's the waiter now."

A different waiter took their order, and once they had tea and pastries in front of them, Waverley's cough suggested he wanted to get on and discuss the death of Dudley Bates.

"I'm sorry to inform you that we have confirmed your suspicion about poisoning, Rachel. Further tests are being carried out as we speak, but it was indeed atropine poisoning that killed Mr Bates."

"I thought it was too bitter to be a useful poison," remarked Sarah.

"It is, and he did react, but from what I can gather from Myra Slade – she's the head of the Murder Mystery Creations company – they wouldn't have suspected anything because it's the same poison they were pretending to use in their fictional murder. They were also drinking a sparkling non-alcoholic dry wine instead of champagne, as Myra didn't want anyone to get drunk."

"Or she didn't want to waste money. And then the fictional murder turned out to be an actual murder," said Rachel. "So clever. If it hadn't been for me mentioning Deadly Nightshade this morning, Sarah would never have cottoned on and we'd be no wiser."

"Precisely," agreed Waverley. "But now we know, so we have to find out who did what."

"Well, that's easy. Pull the footage. They recorded the whole thing live," Rachel suggested.

Waverley coughed again.

"There is no footage?" queried Rachel.

"No. Apparently, it didn't record. A technical glitch."

"Surely you don't believe that?" Marjorie raised her voice.

"No, I don't. But I can't prove anything at the moment. We now have to base our findings on interviews with the cast and observations from last night. That's where you, Rachel, and – erm – you, Lady Marjorie, come in."

"And as actors, they will lie through their teeth and we will be none the wiser," said Rachel, biting into a cinnamon swirl.

"That's about the sum of it. Anyone with access to the stage could have poisoned the drink, and the plant is widely available in the British countryside. It only takes someone who's read up on its toxicity to formulate a dose strong enough to kill."

"But at least we know they had to be on stage after they poured the drinks," Sarah chipped in.

"Yes," agreed Rachel. "And this was a well-planned premeditated murder by someone who had to be familiar with the fictional story and know Act One inside out, which excludes crew and outsiders. We therefore have six suspects with opportunity; all we have to do now is find which one of them has means and a motive strong enough to commit murder. Does Myra Slade know you suspect murder, Chief?"

Waverley slurped his tea, drawing a disparaging look from Marjorie.

"No. I told her I was interviewing her as a matter of routine following the unfortunate death of Mr Bates. I wanted to inform his wife first, but…"

"You'd rather keep the murder under wraps for now and take advantage of our position as murder mystery guests," Rachel suggested.

"Quite. Would you and Lady Marjorie be willing to go ahead and investigate the fictional murder, but surreptitiously investigate the actual murder? I was rather hoping you'd agree to some undercover sleuthing. As long as you realise the fictional killer is likely to differ from the actual killer."

"Oh, do credit us with some intelligence, Chief!" Marjorie snapped.

"I don't believe I'm hearing this conversation. Here we go again. When will you stop treating murder like a game?" Sarah's voice rose a few decibels as she pointedly referred to Marjorie's excitement at becoming embroiled in murder investigations.

Rachel tapped Marjorie's foot under the table, warning her to keep quiet. "Don't worry, Sarah. At least in this case, they won't suspect we know anything is amiss."

"You have three days to help us solve this crime before I tell the actors that one of them is a murderer and begin a formal investigation."

"If the show goes on at all," said Sarah, sulking.

"It is going on. They've all agreed to continue because – as Myra put it – Dudley didn't have an acting part for the rest of the performances, anyway. There's a lot of money involved and she's desperate for a long-term contract with Queen Cruises."

"Cold. She goes to the top of my list," said Marjorie.

"Is his wife all right with continuing the show?" asked Rachel.

"Yes, she is, and if you think Myra's cold, Leanne breathes icicles according to Graham. Goodridge is interviewing her as a matter of formality this afternoon." Waverley shook his head as he spoke.

"She'd be at the top of my list," Sarah added. "She didn't care at all last night when her husband took ill. We had to drag information out of her about his diabetes. My guess is, she knew about his affair with Myra Slade and she wanted to get back at him. Maybe she didn't mean for him to die."

"And, unlike Myra, she was on stage, so could have tampered with the drinks," Rachel concurred.

"While you ask the murder questions, I'll be running background checks on all six of them who were on stage last night. Goodridge and I are speaking to all of the surviving cast members plus Myra under the guise of routine questioning. After all, a passenger has died suddenly. Let me know if you find anything. I've asked Goodridge to meet me later, and then he'll liaise with you after the show in the Jazz Bar."

"What if any of the Creations lot pitch up?" asked Sarah.

"Bring some medical colleagues with you to make it look like you're off duty. I'll tell Goodridge to give you a wide berth if he spots any of them."

"I can't see them being in the Jazz Bar after the show, anyway. They'll be busy packing up, and the mystery passengers will corner those that aren't," said Rachel.

"And please, be careful," Waverley implored as he rose to leave.

"Just one more thing before you go," said Rachel. "Who was in charge of recording last night's show?"

"Myra Slade," said Waverley. "The cruise director offered her our technicians, but she insisted upon it, apparently. Ours set it up, but were only on standby in case she needed them."

"Told you," said Marjorie triumphantly. "It was her."

Chapter 11

Jason Goodridge had struggled to keep awake during his meeting with his boss, Jack Waverley. The long days and occasional nights with little rest in between hit his work-life balance hard at times, and he suffered from periodic bouts of insomnia. Despite being well aware these were caused by repressed memories – that's what the forces' psychologist had told him – from his time in Afghanistan, he had no intention of taking the psychologist's advice and talking about them. Not yet, anyway. Thankful he could survive on short bursts of sleep for most of the time, he knew he just had to ride out the times when his body rebelled.

It had shocked him to hear of the murder of one of the actors from the new show. They had only come on board this voyage – not a brilliant start. Now he had to speak to a seventy-nine-year-old thief. This he wasn't looking forward to one jot.

He called ahead to ask the steward on the eighth floor if Mrs Krystal Brewer was in her room.

"Yes, sir. She's just back from lunch. I made sure her room was cleaned and kept watch on her as instructed. I asked her if she'd like tea when she got back. A pot has just been delivered." Maria, the Filipino stateroom steward, was diligent when asked to do anything. Even better, she was discreet.

"Thanks, Maria, I owe you one. I'm on my way up."

Jason ran up the five flights of stairs to deck eight. The adrenaline had the desired effect of waking him up. He waved to Maria, who was working the corridor, before knocking on the door of room 8337.

"Yes?" The stout woman from the previous night's CCTV footage drew herself up to her full five foot six and held his gaze with heavily eye-lined sky-blue eyes. Spectacles hung on a gold chain around her neck.

"I'm sorry to disturb you, Mrs Brewer. My name is Jason Goodridge, I'm one of the security officers working on board the ship. Would you mind if I asked you a few questions?"

"Security, you say?" She put on her spectacles, poking her head close to his chest to read his badge. "It's a little inconvenient, but you'd better come in."

Great actress, he thought. *Shame Murder Mystery Creations aren't recruiting additional players.*

"I hate to say this, Mrs Brewer, but you were seen leaving room 9860 last night around 9pm."

"Who says?"

"The stateroom steward working that corridor was in the bathroom at the time. He did try to speak to you, but you left in a hurry."

"The stateroom steward is very much mistaken." She held her ground, folding her arms.

"Mrs Brewer, we captured your visit on CCTV footage from the corridor. I can show you on my computer tablet." Jason held up the tablet in his hand.

"You'd better sit down," she huffed. "Spying on guests is not what I expected when I came aboard my first cruise."

Nice move, thought Jason, replying, "We only check footage if we get reports of suspicious activity."

"Okay. So I was there. I made a mistake and entered the wrong room. It must happen all the time. I didn't want anyone thinking I'm a batty old woman."

Jason had expected the wrong room tack. "Please tell me if you took anything from the room and I'll return it. You'll be in less trouble that way."

"What do you mean? Are you insinuating I'm a thief? Did the room holders say I took something?"

"As a matter of fact, they couldn't work out if anything was missing, but you were seen hanging around the corridor until the steward entered that room. You followed him in shortly after and came out a few minutes later. What else would you be doing?"

"That's rather a harsh judgement you've come to, Officer Goodridge. There could be any manner of reasons for my being there. I could be a serial killer, a jealous wife, a lover. Why, I could be an innocent person who went into the wrong room by mistake. You seem a nice young man. Tell me honestly: do I look like a thief?"

The sky-blue eyes held his in an innocent gaze. "No, you don't, but in my experience, looks can be deceptive."

"Rest assured, I'm no thief, and I really was in the wrong room thanks to a stupid receptionist getting their numbers mixed up."

Jason raised an eyebrow. "Mrs Brewer, perhaps you'd better enlighten me. What has a receptionist to do with this?"

"Only if you join me for a cup of tea."

Jason exhaled. Krystal Brewer was a likeable rogue, which wasn't making his job any easier.

"Okay."

Once tea was poured, Mrs Brewer creased up with laughter. "I'm sorry for laughing, but I really have been rather foolish. You see, I'm an actress."

No surprise there, judging by the performance so far, thought Jason.

"One minute, I was meant to be joining this ship as part of a murder mystery troupe. The next, I was told someone else had been cast in my role."

Jason sat bolt upright, suddenly very much awake. "Murder Mystery Creations. You were meant to be working with them?"

"Ah. You've heard of them, then – of course you have, you're security." The old lady took a sip of tea. "Yes, quite right. I had an interview following an audition with the assistant manager, Dudley Bates."

Could this be too much of a coincidence? Jason wasn't certain.

"Dudley told me I had the part, called the manager – Myra Slade, her name is – and confirmed. I let a TV advert for cat food go for that job."

Jason stifled a giggle and slurped his tea back.

"I saw that, Officer. Don't knock it. TV ads pay well when they come up, but this was an opportunity for regular long-term work, an actor's dream. My agent wasn't happy about me finding the job myself; no commission, you see."

"I'm with you so far. I don't suppose your agent's on board?"

"Goodness me! No. I wouldn't be here if he was – he's a worm. Anyway, a week before the cruise, Dudley Bates called and told me his boss had cast someone else instead. As you can imagine, I was furious. Dudley was very apologetic, but told me he couldn't do anything about it. We hadn't signed contracts, so I had no comeback."

"Is that unusual?"

"Not always. Sometimes theatricals aren't the best organised; that's why we have miserable agents. But for a troupe to go back on their word, that is unusual."

"So you decided to take the cruise, anyway. What was your intention?"

"At first, I accepted the knockback as one of those things, but when Demos Benedict – he moonlights with TV ads and we share the same agent – told me Ms Slade had appointed a woman with no acting experience other than amateur dramatics, I saw red. I'm sorry to say, I had an emotional meltdown and booked the cruise. I had a notion that this woman would turn out to be a flop and I'd be on hand to fill her shoes. I contacted Dudley on embarkation day through Demos and he told me I was wasting my time."

Jason poured them both another cup of tea and leaned back. "Whose room did you think you were in last night?"

"The imposter's, of course. I was going to cut up her nightdress and leave a threatening note. Demos told me she's a sensitive soul. I thought it would be enough to send her crying back home."

Jason resisted a smirk. "That would have been a very serious offence, Mrs Brewer."

"I realise that now, and to be honest, I had changed my mind by the time I got inside the room. Too much time hanging around in the corridor, as you put it, gave me the opportunity to think. I don't know why I went in there at all."

"How did you know you were in the wrong room?"

"There were two sets of nightwear, one on each pillow: a rather skimpy negligee and a pair of pyjamas. I ran out as quickly as I could."

Jason did smirk this time. He already knew the names of the couple staying in the stateroom. "I'm happy to say no harm was done. The people in that room are on honeymoon."

"They wouldn't need the nightwear if I'd cut them up, then," Krystal giggled.

"Please, Mrs Brewer, promise me there will be no more shenanigans and we'll close the matter."

"Cross my heart. I really can't be doing with so much excitement at my age. Anyway, I'm pleased I'm not working with them now. I expect you know Dudley Bates died?"

Jason frowned. "We'd rather passengers weren't told anything about the unfortunate death of Mr Bates. I suppose your friend Demos told you."

"Demos is a gossip, a womaniser, and a bit of a drunk. You won't keep him quiet for long. I wouldn't be surprised if he has already told a few of his rich targets."

"What do you mean, targets?"

"He's after a rich woman to keep him and give him the lavish life he craves. He told me this morning he had found someone who might fit the bill. She's about seventeen years older than him."

Jason's jaw dropped.

"You're shocked, Officer Goodridge. You shouldn't be. It makes sense if you're him. Find a rich woman. Get her to feel safe in his wandering arms, burn money while she lives and inherit a fortune on her death. He tends to go for older women, anyway."

Jason felt sick to the stomach. Not necessarily about the age difference, but by the callousness of the man's plan.

"Who is this poor woman?"

"I don't know. He could be making it up. He likes to think he's God's gift. I'm sure you meet a lot of his type on cruise ships. From what I hear, they're rife with opportunists looking to bag themselves a fortune."

"I hate to disappoint, Mrs Brewer, but that's not my experience."

"Call me Krystal, please."

"Thank you, Krystal, for the tea. I hope I won't be needing to speak to you again in my professional capacity. I suggest you enjoy the cruise and stay away from the Murder Mystery Creations group."

"I promise I'll be good, Officer Goodridge."

"Just one more question. How did you find Dudley Bates?"

"How was his health, you mean? He looked unhealthy to me: pale beneath the false tan, overweight with a beer gut and a chain smoker. Not just cigarettes, if you ask me. Why do you ask?"

Ignoring the question, Jason pressed, "Did you like him?"

Krystal hesitated while she collected her thoughts. "Yes, I'd say I did like him. He was affable, but there was a sadness behind those eyes. Are you thinking he did himself in?"

"No, we're not thinking that. Thank you for your time, Krystal. Please stay out of trouble."

Jason was putting all the pieces together and concluded Krystal was telling the truth. He was annoyed a receptionist had given out a guest's room number, even if it was the wrong one, but it wasn't top of his priority list. He couldn't help liking the troublesome Krystal Brewer and hoped rather than believed she would keep her word.

Chapter 12

The Cocktail Lounge was buzzing with excitement by the time Rachel and Marjorie arrived for round two of 'Murder on Deck'. Myra and some of the actors were mixing with crowds of passengers who were lining up to quiz them on the events of the previous night, unaware that an actual murder had taken place.

"I'm rather surprised the good Chief Waverley isn't interviewing any of the passengers whilst the events of last night are fresh in their minds," remarked Marjorie.

The same thought had occurred to Rachel. Despite using the element of surprise in letting the murderer believe they had got away with it, he was taking a tremendous risk. The longer he left it, the more likely people would not remember facts accurately. Memories of events would fade as the days passed by.

"Puts the onus on us, doesn't it?" she replied.

"Yes, it does."

"Perhaps he's relying on the fact people will make notes. I spotted quite a few writing during last night's performance."

"Now that makes sense. But I do hope he's not putting too much responsibility on your shoulders. These people pretend for a living."

"*Our* shoulders. You're in on this, too, remember?"

Marjorie's eyes lit up at the inclusion. Rachel hoped they could get to the bottom of this mystery sooner rather than later. She cast her eyes around the room as people took cocktails and chatted. The assembled waiters would serve dinner after the second cocktail reception.

"I'll help as much as I can," said Marjorie. "I suppose we'd better get on with it, then. Do you think we should split up?"

"Good idea. I want to tackle Myra, although strictly speaking she's not one of the actors. I could quiz her on what happens next and why the reruns aren't being shown, see if she gives anything away."

"Mario told me he'd enquired and been told 'technical error' just like His Lordship said." Marjorie's nickname for Chief Waverley had stuck, and even Rachel thought of him in the same terms at times.

"Who are you going to aim for so we don't duplicate?"

"I'll take on the womaniser, Demos, save you the blather. I think I'll also try Nellie Hurst, who acted as the lounge singer. We don't know much about her yet. If I don't get anywhere, I could always ask her for advice on Botox," Marjorie chuckled. "No point trying to speak to the bashful Cody again, I don't suppose."

"Not for now. No, he won't have anything else to say. Right, I'll take Myra and Gladys Knott and, if there's time, Leanne Bates."

"Don's wife?"

"Dudley's wife."

Marjorie giggled. "Just checking," she teased. "If you don't get the opportunity, we can nab her after the show this evening. Despite what His Lordship said, I'm surprised to see her here. She really didn't care for her husband, did she?"

"It would appear not. We've got forty-five minutes before dinner, so I'll catch you later."

Rachel hung around a group of people surrounding Myra Slade, listening in on the conversation while she waited for her opportunity. Tonight, Myra had taken power dressing to the next level, wearing a cream knee-length skirt buttoned down the front and open at the bottom, a light tan silk blouse tucked in at the waist and tan six-inch-heeled shoes. The fashionably dyed white hair sported a side fringe with the rest trimmed neatly around the ears. She wore gold pearl drop earrings and a gold chain around her neck.

"This is our first show on a cruise liner. No matter how much I prepare for all eventualities, sometimes things go wrong, especially when I have to rely on outsiders."

Taking no responsibility there, then, thought Rachel.

"I've worked hard to retrieve the audio, but alas, the video footage has completely disappeared. The equipment can't have been set up properly." Myra cast a cursory glance towards technicians preparing the stage, as if by doing so, she would ensure people would understand she had to work with inferior labour.

"Never mind, Jo-Jo always takes notes. He's also got some footage on his cell phone." A petite woman with an American accent spoke, but was ignored as Myra was listening to a taller woman with a louder voice. Rachel kicked herself inwardly. Of course! Some people would record videos, despite being asked not to before the show started.

She sidled over to the short woman who had been unceremoniously pushed aside by the tall woman and her even taller husband or partner. They had now commandeered Myra's attention, but rather than ask questions, they were giving their account of how they had worked out who the killer was. Myra listened politely, giving nothing away.

"I'm afraid I can't tell you whether you're right or wrong. All will be revealed in due course. Let's see if you still have the same person down as chief suspect after tonight's performance."

The petite woman waited, obviously put out at being pushed aside and remaining determined to speak to Myra.

"I heard you say you're with someone who took notes. What a good idea. I didn't think to do that." Rachel smiled down at the woman who appeared to be aged around seventy, dressed in a scarlet cocktail dress fitting neatly into the curves of her slight frame. She had a beautiful open face.

"Jo-Jo, that's my husband. He's over there quizzing the duchess." Rachel followed the other woman's eyes towards an older man with short white hair and a white moustache, dressed in a brown suit and leaning into a brown walking cane. He was speaking to Gladys Knott, who was smiling.

"He's doing well, I think. He seems to have the duchess smiling."

"Oh, Jo-Jo can get people to open up in an instant. It's a gift. He's disarming, but sharp as a button. Actually, he was a police officer before he got shot in the knee and was forced to retire. He loves these things."

"Have you been to many? It's my first time."

"We've not been to one on a cruise ship before or one by this company – they're British, but we go to a few back home. It was going well until the video didn't appear. We hate things like that. Jo-Jo thinks it's suspicious and asked me to find out about it. I'm not getting very far, as you can see." The woman glared at her usurper's back. It didn't look like she would be moving anytime soon. "I'm Celia May, by the way."

"Rachel. Rachel Jacobi-Prince. Pleased to meet you."

"I love that English accent of yours. You remind me of our granddaughter. She loves murder mysteries, too. She's followed in the footsteps of her granddaddy, much to our son's dismay."

"Whereabouts in America are you from?"

"We're from Florida. The sunshine state. I guess you've heard of it?"

Rachel nodded. Celia May was an interesting woman, and she and her husband could be useful when it came to the investigation. Rachel lowered her voice.

"Why does your husband think the loss of the video is suspicious?"

"I'm not sure. He says it's just a hunch, but his hunches tend to be right. Next thing you know, he'll be investigating an actual murder. Homicide was his bag when he was in the police. I just wish he'd relax more. He misses his job so much. It wasn't just a job to him, it was his life. Still, he relives it vicariously through Annie – that's our granddaughter."

Rachel glanced over at the short, unassuming man who was still talking to Gladys Knott. The older woman appeared completely taken up by Jo-Jo. Would he get too close to the real killer? An uncomfortable knot formed in Rachel's stomach as concern for the older man hit her like a brick.

***

Celia May and Rachel eventually gave up their attempts to speak with Myra Slade as the ignorant couple continued to dominate both physically and verbally. Myra did not try to move them on, despite others waiting to speak to her.

"Jo-Jo's heading off to speak to the duchess's sister now. I'm giving up here." Celia May looked down at a note in her hand. "I'll go and have a chat with the waiter, Todd. He's a shy-looking fella."

"He is. My friend and I spoke to him earlier. His actual name's Cody and he's the son of the woman who plays the duchess, Gladys Knott."

"I thank you for the extra information. It's been a pleasure, Rachel. Hope to see you around the ship. I'd love to introduce you to Jo-Jo."

And I'd love to meet him, thought Rachel. "I'd like that," she said. "I'm going to grab the duchess while she's free." She squeezed Celia May's arm before heading in the direction of Gladys Knott.

Gladys forced a smile as Rachel approached. "Hello."

"Good evening, Duchess. I wonder if I might ask you some questions about last night?"

"Of course," Gladys Knott was well and truly into her role, but her arrogant air seemed real. Her eyes bored into the back of the man who had just departed.

Hands off, he's married, thought Rachel, but said, "Would you mind telling me a little about your relationship with your sister, Dora?"

Gladys's head shot round and her piercing blue eyes fixed on Rachel's, glaring at her, clearly unhappy at having to take her gaze off Jo-Jo. "I was expecting you to ask what I saw and heard prior to the murder."

"I'm sure we'll get to that, but for now, I was just wondering why you don't get on with your sister. There was a lot of tension between the two of you."

"She's a whore, if you must know. Sleeps around with anything in trousers. No wonder her husband played away from home."

"She appears very loyal to you. How long's she been your secretary?"

"What? Oh yes. She's worked for me for twenty years. Useless at her job."

"And yet you keep her on. Why?"

"Because she knows things about the family."

"Are you worried she might tell others about these things?"

"Perhaps. But I know a lot more about her. I've been digging. She's just a two-bit whore and her husband's no better."

Rachel decided it was time to strike. "But I thought your sister was single?" Rachel's original question had clearly thrown Gladys, who seemed to be giving her opinion about Leanne Bates rather than the character she was playing, Dora Michaels.

Gladys looked as though someone had hit her. "Oh yes, my sister is single. Weren't you asking about Toni Cleeves, the lounge singer?"

Good recovery, thought Rachel. "So it's Toni who sleeps around, not your sister, Dora?"

"Yes, that's right."

"And what about your relationship with the dead man?"

"I didn't have a relationship with him."

"But wasn't he your nephew?"

"I'm sorry, young lady, I'm feeling rather tired. Do you think you could go now?" Gladys waved a dismissive hand, imagining it would shuffle Rachel away, but she stood her ground. "Cody! I don't feel well."

Rachel turned to see that Cody and Myra were sharing an intimate moment nearby. He pivoted at the sound of his mother's voice, leaving Myra and scurrying towards her. Gladys clung to her son, feigning dizziness.

"It's all right, Mother. I'm here. What happened?" he asked Rachel.

"I'm not certain. I was quizzing her in her fictional role as the duchess about the character, Dora Michaels. She appeared to be confusing fact and fiction, and then she had a funny turn." Rachel neglected to say it happened when Gladys saw Cody embracing Myra Slade.

"I see, well, she's not used to acting. Didn't we meet earlier?" He didn't wait for a reply and turned back to his mother. "Perhaps you've had enough for now, Mother. Let's get you a drink."

"That might help." The old woman recovered enough to steer her son away with a vicelike grip from the oncoming Myra Slade. A scowl crossed Myra's face as her lips tightened. Rachel took her chance.

"Hello, I'm Rachel. Could I ask you a question about what happened to the video reruns from last night? My friend and I have been trying to catch up with it all day."

Myra rolled her eyes and sighed heavily before pulling herself together. "I'm afraid there was a technical hitch, so we only have audio. I'll explain all about it when I introduce this evening's show. Were you with Dr Knott just now?"

"I was with Gladys Knott – is she a doctor? I didn't know that," Rachel felt a white lie wouldn't hurt under the circumstances.

"She was. She's retired now, but likes to be referred to as Doctor."

"And now she's taken up acting, I see." Rachel pretended to sound impressed.

"Not really. We have an older actress who's part of the team, but she's frightened of sailing – gets seasick – Dr Knott offered to stand-in once she knew her son was joining the cruise. I wanted to get a proper actress, but Cody persuaded me to take her on." A bitter tone crept into Myra's otherwise controlled voice.

Not the way Cody tells it, thought Rachel. "I see. Well, she was exceptional playing the part of the duchess last night. It's as if she was born to it."

"Mm. I suppose all those years of being a consultant, lording it over people, help. Doctors make excellent actors, you know. All those lies they tell us over the years." Myra burst into giggles, but the laughter didn't reach the eyes.

Rachel laughed along politely. "I suppose it must help. I'm afraid she gets confused about the characters, though."

Myra's right eyebrow rose. "Oh?"

"Yes. I was asking her about her relationship with her fictional sister and she confused her with someone who was married and slept around. I thought the duchess's sister was meant to be single." At that moment, Rachel realised that policewomen also made excellent actresses.

"Yes, she is. What did she say?"

"Something about the woman being a whore and it was no wonder her husband slept around." Rachel noted the flicker of a reaction cross Myra's forehead and the lips tightened once more.

"I don't think we have a character like that."

"Oh? She said she was confusing her fictional sister with the lounge singer, played by Nellie Hurst, I believe?"

"No. Toni's husband – fictional husband – is a night watchman, and neither of them sleep around according to the script."

"Are you sure?"

"Of course I'm sure! I wrote the blooming thing. Now, if you'll excuse me, I'd better check up on Cody… Dr Knott, I mean."

Rachel found herself staring at the back of Myra as the older woman turned abruptly and headed backstage.

Chapter 13

Rachel approached Leanne Bates who, considering her husband had died last night, appeared to be in remarkably good humour. She and a group of four passengers were laughing at something one of the men had said.

While she waited for them to finish their conversation, which appeared to have more to do with the jocular man's antics at previous Creations events than the current murder mystery, Rachel checked her notes again. Leanne had played the part of Dora Michaels, the duchess's sister-cum-secretary, and had suffered hostile abuse from her imaginary sister in her role. The performance had implied the duchess believed Dora was there to be used and abused. It would probably turn out to be something to do with money, but Leanne's acting part wasn't what interested Rachel.

Finally, the group said their goodbyes, and Rachel was next in line to speak with Leanne. The woman's hazel eyes slanted as Rachel introduced herself. Close up, Leanne appeared older than the forty years Rachel had read in the brochure. A chiffon scarf covered the birthmark on her neck and the dress she wore provided a flattering disguise to the straight down apple-shaped body. She wore an auburn wig, the same one she had been wearing in her stage part, and Rachel mused she would be attractive if she didn't set her face in a permanent scowl.

Thin lips forced a smile as Leanne held out her hand to shake Rachel's. Rachel glanced at the acrylic nails that felt sharp as they shook hands.

"We're pressed for time and don't have long before dinner, so please ask any questions you have." Leanne's opening remarks were as sharp as her nails and a far cry from the tone she'd displayed with the previous group.

"Okay. Did you place the Deadly Nightshade poison in Marvin Black's drink? I noticed you were close to the bar where he went to fetch it himself."

Leanne sucked in her bottom lip and her eyes narrowed further.

"You're very observant, Miss…"

"Mrs… Mrs Jacobi-Prince, but call me Rachel." Rachel smiled while the woman in front of her gathered herself together.

"Well, Rachel, you obviously haven't been to one of these events before, or read the rules. You're not allowed to ask any of the cast if they are the murderer." She continued with the same condescending tone, obviously rattled by Rachel's question, "You may ask where I was, or for my opinion on any of the others, but as I said, we're running out of time." Leanne stifled a yawn.

Rude as well as cold, thought Rachel. "My mistake. Perhaps you could tell me about your relationship with Marvin instead. Were you in love with him?"

If Leanne's eyes narrowed any further, they would be tight shut. She cackled loudly, causing others waiting to speak to her to halt their conversations.

"Whatever makes you think that?"

Rachel stood tall and held the woman's gaze. "Apologies, but as you're seemingly a stickler for the rules, I'm supposed to ask the questions and you're meant to answer."

Leanne stopped laughing, sucked in her bottom lip and glared at Rachel. "No. I can assure you I was not in love with Dudley… erm, Marvin Black. He was a waster and a drug addict. I don't know what I saw in him in the first place."

Rachel jumped in immediately. "So you were in love with him in the past?"

"This conversation's over," snarled Leanne. "Next!" She turned away from Rachel and summoned the people behind with her hand. The next couple hurried towards the so-called actress, barely noticing the abrupt dismissal of Rachel, who wasn't done yet.

"Thank you for your time, Mrs Bates. It must be hard to separate fact from fiction when working with your husband."

Rachel felt Leanne's eyes boring into her back as she strolled towards the dinner table where she would meet Marjorie. Enid and Kate were already seated when she arrived. She ordered a Martini and lemonade from the waiter who had just finished taking orders from her two table companions.

"Hello. Did you have a good day?" asked Kate.

"Yes, thank you. And you?"

"We did. Mum and I met Demos for lunch, and then went for pampering sessions at the spa. It's a shame about the video rerun's not working. Demos says there was a technical hitch. I hope it hasn't put you off. They're normally very professional."

"These things happen. In a way, it makes it more intriguing. I've just been quizzing some of the cast. Leanne Bates seems out of sorts. She didn't want to answer any of my questions. Is she always like that?"

The exchange of glances between the two women told her that Demos had most likely been indiscreet. They almost certainly knew Dudley Bates was dead.

"She can be uptight at the best of times," offered Enid. "I think she's got a lot on her mind. She's quite ambitious."

"Driven, more like," added Kate. "She wants a controlling interest in Murder Mystery Creations, from what we've heard. She and her husband invested a large sum of money recently and own a forty-eight per cent share in the company."

Rachel processed this additional information. Perhaps Enid and Kate didn't know about Dudley's death after all.

"I wouldn't want her as an enemy," she said. "I imagine she could be quite ruthless if she wanted to be."

"You've got wonderful insight. It took us ages to work out the truth behind the lives of our actors and actresses. I'd say we know them all pretty well now. Leanne's the only one I can't take to." Enid looked at her daughter, who nodded in agreement.

"Insight or not, I don't seem to be getting very far with this murder. The off-screen characters with all their quirks are distracting. You're right about Leanne being awkward; it's a shame because she could be quite attractive behind the offensive exterior."

"I don't know why Myra continues to work with her. It must be to do with the money she and Dudley invested. They don't get on at all. I'm sure Leanne knows about the affair Mum mentioned last night."

"I suspect Myra's regretting their financial arrangement now. She promoted Dudley on the back of the investment, and most likely while he and Myra were together. Demos was sidestepped from a well-deserved promotion," Enid added, face flushing.

The announcement that the waiters would serve dinner imminently, directing passengers to return to their tables, came over the microphone. Rachel didn't have any opportunity to follow up the latest piece of information, but wondered if Marjorie had managed to draw anything from Demos. If she knew Marjorie, she was certain she would have.

***

Marjorie found Demos at the edge of the Cocktail Lounge, downing what looked like a large whisky.

"May I intrude?" she asked.

His brown eyes turned to her and he stood straight. "It's no intrusion. How can I help, Mrs…?"

"Lady Marjorie Snellthorpe. I'm a widow, I'm afraid."

Pound signs clearly totted up in the young man's head as he took her hand and brought it up to his lips while fixing her eyes with his.

"I'm so sorry to hear that. I'm Demos Benedict, actor, at your service."

"I have to say, I thought you were marvellous as the grandson, Sly Toner, last night. It must be an exciting life, being an actor."

Demos took Marjorie's arm and steered her with him towards a waiter. He placed his empty glass on a tray and took two cocktails, handing her one.

"It can be. A company offered me a lucrative contract before I joined this cruise." His face darkened.

"I'm not surprised, a man of your talent and with your looks. Was it film or television?"

"It was theatre, but with a view to a television deal later on."

"And will you be starting your new contract when you return from this event?"

Pouting his lips like a spoilt teenager, he spluttered, "I turned it down."

"Oh dear. Why would you do that?"

"Because I was under the impression – no, *promised* a promotion to assistant manager, but she went back on her word." He downed his cocktail in one gulp and clicked his fingers at a passing waitress.

Marjorie held back her irritation at his bad manners. "You say 'she'. Are you referring to Myra Slade?" Marjorie glanced around to find Demos had now led her close to a doorway where waiters came in and out with their newly laden trays. No-one could overhear the conversation.

"Yes, her. She gave the job to her boyfriend, that was. Two months after, she meets another loser, Cody Spark – he's a wuss, right mummy's boy – and then she dumps Dudley Bates, the guy who played Marvin Black. After that, she treats him like dirt."

"I'm sorry. You're losing me. Perhaps you could start from the beginning. I'm a good listener."

Demos's bloodshot eyes settled on Marjorie again, and he held her hand for longer than she felt comfortable with. She was at the point of extracting it when he let go.

"You are a good listener, Lady Snellthorpe, but I don't want to burden you with my troubles. You're on holiday and you probably want to quiz me about last night."

"Oh, there's plenty of time for that. It wouldn't be a burden at all. It doesn't sound fair what has happened to you. Sometimes sharing a problem helps you feel better about it and offers a solution. Besides, I have contacts in the film business."

"You do?" His face lit up and his eyes registered 'Jackpot'.

"Tell me what happened and I'll see if there's anything I can help you with."

"Myra Slade – she's the woman who owns and started Murder Mystery Creations – is ambitious and driven; you know the sort. I've been with her for ten years now, almost as long as she's had the company. I've worked hard and asked for nothing in return. The company's growth has gone through the roof over the past few years with the popularity of these high-end murder mystery weekends – sometimes an entire week. When she got this cruise contract, she decided she needed an assistant manager who would be in charge of the cruise arm of the business. If this goes well – and there's every reason for it to do so… well, there was, anyway. We've had a few minor hitches."

"Such as?"

"I'll come on to that, but not long after she got this gig, she promised me the job. Then she had an affair with someone else in the team. A married man, not that his wife cared. She puts it about a bit herself. Anyway, four months before this cruise, Myra promotes him – Dudley – out of the blue. No warning, nothing. We were just informed that it was a done deal." Demos paused to down another cocktail.

"Did you challenge her about her promise?"

"Yes. We argued. I told her she had promised me the job. She told me it was her company and she could do what she liked. She made the excuse that the company needed investment and Dudley and his wife had money. Acted like I didn't know he was in her pants."

"Well, the money part could be true. Businesses that are expanding need extra investment."

Demos pouted again. "I s'pose they do, but that's not the point. She promised. It's not fair."

Marjorie resisted the temptation to explain to this rather immature man who must be pushing forty that life was sometimes unfair.

"So what happened next?"

"A couple of months later, once the money was in and she'd ensconced Dudley as assistant manager, she tired of him. She always tires of her conquests."

Marjorie suspected Demos may have slept his way to the promise of promotion at an earlier juncture. "And?"

"She meets Cody and tells everyone he's the real thing – it's pathetic. Now the joke's on her 'cos it appears she is in love with this spineless geek, but like I said, he's a mummy's boy. Everyone can see that his mummy will never let him marry Myra." He spat out the words.

"How sad."

"It would be if she wasn't such a witch. She's only getting what she deserves."

"Now, let me get this straight. Myra has an affair with Dudley – I assume that's Dudley Bates who played Marvin Black, the one who died last night—"

"Yep, he died all right."

Marjorie ignored the interruption for the time being. "She then promotes this Dudley in exchange for an investment in her business. You believe his wife knows about the affair, but doesn't really care as she's not the faithful type either."

"Yup. Got it so far. You're quick, Lady Snellthorpe, I'm impressed." He reached for her hand again, but she managed to clasp it around her drink, cupping the cocktail with both hands.

"Then she meets Cody, falls in love, dumps Dudley, and now she's in trouble because her new love's mother is going to do everything she can to tear them apart. Does that sound about right?"

"You missed out the bit about her breaking her promise to me, but yeah, that just about sums it up. She treated Dud – that's what we call him, 'cos he was a dud, a fake – treated him like dirt after she dumped him. He still had a torch for her, if you know what I mean, but she despised him once their fling was over, and she hates his wife. I think she was trying to buy them out."

"So they invested as a couple, then?"

"Yeah, I think so." He looked around for the next waiter, clicking his fingers again before helping himself.

"Did you say Dudley *had* a torch for her? Has he gone off her again?"

"He's gone off, all right. You see, Lady Snellthorpe, Dudley Bates really died after the show last night. Ironic, isn't it?"

Marjorie feigned a jaw drop. "Oh, how tragic!"

Demos pulled himself upright, realising he must sound callous. "Yeah, it is sad. He wasn't in the best of health, though. Too much drink, and he did drugs."

He's not the only one who drinks too much. Marjorie left this unsaid as the announcement came from the stage, asking guests to join their tables for dinner and calling the cast backstage.

"Better go, she doesn't like any of us to be late. We should talk again, Lady Snellthorpe. I'd love to hear more about your contacts."

"But won't you be in line for the assistant manager's job again? Once the dust settles, as it were."

Demos frowned. "I thought so. Now she says she's not sure; seems it was all for nothing."

Marjorie stared after him, wondering what he was referring to. Did Demos kill Dudley in order to get the job?

Chapter 14

After dinner, Tatum Rodman took to the stage as she had on the previous night. "Thank you so much to all of you for your forbearance over the past twenty-four hours. As you may have gathered, or been told, we haven't been able to provide the reruns of last night's 'Murder on Deck' Act One. As a token of goodwill for the inconvenience, Queen Cruises has agreed to apply $50 onboard credit to each one of your accounts. Rest assured, we have now unearthed the issue, and we have rectified it.

"Myra Slade, CEO of Murder Mystery Creations, has worked hard all day to provide you with an outline summary of what happened during last night's scene and you will have access to the audio recording via your stateroom TV. During dinner, you will be given copies of the summary to peruse, and the next four acts will be recorded by Murder Mystery Creations *and* by our own theatre technicians to ensure there will be no further mishaps. I'm sure you'll agree murder is enough of a conundrum without technical issues. One would be forgiven for thinking it was deliberate."

Laughter filled the room, but Rachel could see Myra standing at the side of the stage with a face that would melt ice.

"Now, please enjoy your dinner. There will be half an hour after dinner where you can avail yourself of the facilities, request drinks and so on before Act Two, which begins at 8pm. Remember, we will be in port tomorrow, so enjoy your day either on land or on board the *Coral Queen* and I'll see you again tomorrow evening for Act Three." Applause followed the assistant cruise director as she left the stage.

After dinner Rachel nodded towards the door. She and Marjorie excused themselves from Enid and Kate, who were avidly reading the notes that had been handed out during dinner. Once outside, Rachel took Marjorie's arm and they found seats at a table for two affording a night-time view of the North Sea. They were on a busy shipping lane and could see lights from other ships in the distance.

Rachel related her encounters with the three women and each of their reactions. "Gladys was totally muddled. I think she was referring to Dudley's affair with Myra when she went off on one about his wife being a whore. She doesn't approve of Myra, either."

"None of them sound at all pleasant. I wonder why they were so rude to you."

"I obviously prodded a little too hard. Gladys was disappointed that an elderly man she'd been laughing with left her, and I just happened to be next. Then she couldn't take her eyes off her son. Myra had obviously escaped the crowd and found him. She told me Gladys was the one who volunteered to take the part – different to what Cody said this afternoon."

"That's odd, but not surprising. From the sounds of it, she wouldn't want her darling son alone in the clutches of the enigmatic Myra Slade. I expect he doesn't realise. And Myra wouldn't dare refuse the woman in case she persuaded the precious Cody to stay home. Myra's in love with him, according to Demos."

"Oh?"

"What about Myra? Did you get much out of her and do you think she tampered with the equipment?"

"We won't know that until we find out what the issue was. We'll need to ask Sarah."

"Why Sarah?"

"She knows the assistant cruise director well, and the latter is friends with Myra – although after tonight, she might not be."

Marjorie giggled. "She did hit rather close to the mark, didn't she? Myra's annoyance could be at the suggestion of guilt."

"Or pride. She's not the sort to suffer fools and I can't see her tolerating incompetence. She's already shown she's a control freak in that she wants to record everything herself."

"Control freak or murderer?"

"Don't worry, I haven't ruled her out yet, but let's face it: Leanne Bates has to be the coldest widow I've ever come across. She's behaving as if nothing's happened."

"Not to mention, you don't like her," Marjorie suggested.

"You're right there. I don't like her at all, and Enid and Kate confirmed she's nasty. They think she wants controlling interest in the company. She and the deceased own forty-eight per cent."

"I knew they had invested. That much I found out from Demos Benedict. He drinks too much, by the way. Also, he has motive."

Marjorie told her about her conversation with Demos before dinner and all he'd revealed.

"I'm afraid I didn't get the chance to speak to Nellie Hurst."

"Sounds like you got a fair bit of information from Demos, though. He sounds like a spoilt opportunistic brat." Rachel was pleased to hear of Demos's flaws, as it helped her dispel any likeness the handsome man had to her own Carlos.

"He is all of that and more, and of course he's got a loose tongue. Talk about woe is me. He needs a good shake, but his interest in all of this can't be disregarded. He resented Don taking his so-called promised job."

"Dudley," Rachel corrected.

"Yes, Dudley. While he was having the affair with Myra, she gave him an assistant management position that, according to Demos, he had been promised."

"Do you believe him?"

"Only if he had slept with Myra. Otherwise, no-one in their right mind would consider him for promotion. He's too unstable and, as I said, he drinks far too much."

"Did he sleep with Myra?"

"Oh, I would imagine he did; he's a male slut, willing to sleep his way to whatever he can get. He even flirted with me! Particularly after I told him I knew people in the film business and might be able to help him with his career."

"Marjorie Snellthorpe! That reminds me of the time you pretended to be arranging my birthday party with that Queen tribute act."

"It worked then, and it worked tonight. He was all for revealing everything, although one would need to separate fact from fiction because I suspect he embellishes the truth. It's a pity we didn't get to speak for longer. The fact is, he hated Dudley, and isn't fond of the man's wife either. He could be our man."

"So we have Myra with no obvious motive, unless Dudley had some information he was blackmailing her with. Leanne has motive because of the affair, but doesn't seem to have cared enough for her late husband to go off into a fit of jealous rage. Although she might have wanted him out of the way so she can enact her takeover ambitions on her own. Then there's Cody, who doesn't have a motive unless he found out about Dudley and Myra and killed him – I can't see it, to be honest; too weak. Cody's mother resents his involvement with Myra Slade, but if anything, she'd have been happy for Dudley to rekindle Myra's fire, from what Demos told you. She's unlikely to let things get serious between Myra and Cody, but she has no motive for killing Dudley. As for Demos, resenting a man's promotion and murder don't amount to the same thing. He's a bit too pathetic, from what you've said, and the way he hangs around Enid and Kate – he's a womaniser, definitely, but a killer?"

"He is rather weak. And all too ready to put on a sympathy party. I suspect he'd be a little more circumspect if he was our killer. Some poor unsuspecting rich woman will fall for his act and he'll land on his feet. I hope it isn't Enid; I like her."

"She's tempted, I'm sure, but I bet in her saner moments she can see through Mr Demos Benedict. I don't think she's stupid enough to do anything rash."

"What about Kate? She's besotted."

"Hopefully Enid will keep her from harm. Anyway, I suspect Enid's the one with the money, so Kate won't be the one he's after. Besides," Rachel nudged Marjorie and chuckled, "he likes older women."

"There's life in this old bird yet," Marjorie huffed, laughing as they returned to the Cocktail Lounge.

***

Rachel studied the evening's performance in every detail. Would the fictional murderer turn out to be the real killer? Was this person foolish or genius enough to have turned a fictional murder into a real-life one where they would be found out and arrested on stage for the acted one, whilst getting away with the real one? It was highly unlikely, but this was not an ordinary murderer she was dealing with. This person considered themselves so clever, they committed a murder in front of almost a hundred witnesses.

One thing Rachel was certain of: their killer was arrogant. She hoped the arrogance would be their downfall and she didn't want to miss any clues, even if what she was watching at present was staged.

Each person played their part well, as they had done on the previous evening. Someone she hadn't met before played the ship's security chief, who was investigating the crime.

"Who's that man playing the chief?" asked Marjorie.

"Demos told us they meant Dudley to play him, but he has… erm… taken ill, so the part's being played by someone from the onboard theatre crew," Enid explained.

So you do know Dudley's dead, Rachel mused.

"It must have been the poison," joked Marjorie.

"What poison?" asked Kate, paling.

"Oh, Rachel here believes the killer committed the murder using Deadly Nightshade. Methinks Myra Slade – or whoever wrote this play – has read a little too much Agatha Christie."

"We thought that too, didn't we, Mum?"

Enid didn't appear to be listening. Her thoughts were clearly far away as she gazed towards Demos, taking to the stage in his role as the duchess's petulant grandson. *Close to the truth*, Rachel thought. Kate's eyes followed her mother's, and she too became mesmerised.

Marjorie frowned. Rachel hoped the infatuation wouldn't cause a breakup in what appeared to be a healthy and close mother-daughter relationship. She exchanged a glance with Marjorie, who was clearly thinking along similar lines.

Unlike in the actual murder, each person on stage appeared to have a motive. The chief confirmed that poison had been found in the victim's body and explained how easy it would be to kill someone with a dose of the common plant, if the person took a large enough swig at once.

"You see, the poison is extremely bitter and the victim would realise something was amiss. In this case, the killer gave our victim a fatal dose in a glass of champagne. The murderer would have known our victim's tendency to knock back booze and would have been assured the dose was enough to kill." The chief was explaining his theory to Sly Toner, who had the least-known motive for the murder. The death of the duchess's nephew wouldn't increase his share of the inheritance, which would pass to her sister.

Ironic, thought Rachel, as Leanne would inherit Dudley's wealth in real life.

The audience paid particular attention to this part of the spiel and many took notes. Rachel saw out of the corner of her eye the ex-police officer whose wife, Celia May, she'd met earlier. They were seated with their backs to the wall and he was taking copious notes while his wife filmed surreptitiously with a mobile phone. Rachel made a mental note to find out more about Jo-Jo and get Waverley to warn him off before he put himself or his wife in danger.

The show ended with a few more clues, mainly pointing towards the duchess's sister being the guilty party.

"I'm pleased that's over. I've got a headache from concentrating." Marjorie raised her voice to be heard above the applause. "Should I try to corner Nellie Hurst before we leave?"

"No, I'm tired, too," Rachel called back over the noise. "Are you up to meeting Sarah in the Jazz Bar, or would you rather give it a miss?"

"Oh yes, I am. Besides, I haven't had my after-dinner brandy. I was saving myself."

"Come on, then. Let's make a quick exit before everyone else does the same." Rachel waved to Enid and Kate. "We'll see you tomorrow. Enjoy your day out."

Enid waved back, but Kate was still clapping rapturously with her eyes on Demos.

Once they arrived at the Jazz Bar, Rachel saw Sarah was already there, tucked away in a booth where they had regularly met up in the past to discuss cases. Bernard and Brigitte were also there. Rachel didn't mind seeing Bernard, but Brigitte hated discussions about murder, preferring to pretend nothing was amiss.

"I haven't seen Sarah's fiancé, Jason. They haven't fallen out, have they?" Marjorie remarked.

"Not as far as I know," Rachel laughed. "You can ask her, if you like."

"I will do no such thing, but I will ask when we might see him."

Sarah and her fiancé, Jason Goodridge, had finally settled on a wedding date for the spring when their current nine-month contracts expired. They planned to take a three-month break before returning to cruise ship life. Rachel was looking forward to meeting up with them in England. Carlos and Jason got on well and, with their military backgrounds, were good for each other.

"Hello, you two. How was the second act?" Sarah asked.

Rachel and Marjorie shuffled alongside Sarah on the bench, and Bernard and Brigitte sat opposite.

"Tiring, if you must know," said Rachel. "It's difficult trying to untangle two mysteries while trying not to confuse them inside your head."

"Did you have that problem too? I thought it was my ageing brain. It really is too much. I'm mixing up the characters with the actors and coming up with many scenarios. The ones we're being fed, and the ones based on reality."

"I'm sure you'll work it out." Bernard sat back, grinning. "You always do. It was worse for me. I had to see that demanding woman again before the show."

"What woman?" asked Marjorie.

Bernard rolled his eyes and looked heavenwards. "Gladys Knott. I'm not meant to call her by her first name – in the middle of a so-called fainting attack, she found the ability to tell me to refer to her as Doctor Knott." He raised his eyebrows before laughing.

"I'm afraid I was the one who set her off," said Rachel. "I was quizzing her about her role in the play and she got her characters muddled."

"So I have you to blame. In that case, you can buy me a drink."

"With pleasure," said Rachel. "Although the whole situation worsened when the good lady noticed her son in an intimate embrace with Myra Slade, the manager of the Creations group."

"Ah, you're only half responsible, so I'll take a half pint." Bernard giggled. Brigitte scowled at her mischievous colleague.

"Don't you dare buy him a drink, Rachel. He owes us a round."

"She's right, it's my turn to buy. I'll get you ladies a drink – Stingers, perhaps?"

"Not unless you want another death on your hands," laughed Rachel. As well as being a merciless tease, Bernard was the creator of an infamous secret cocktail that was to be avoided on fear of death, according to Sarah and Brigitte.

"I won't hear of Stingers and I won't take your money; you need it to send home to your family. I'm buying," Marjorie chipped in. "And you, young man, will behave yourself."

Chapter 15

Rachel spotted Jason heading towards them and beamed. She stood to hug him. "Marjorie and I have been wondering where you were."

Jason hugged Rachel back and leaned down to kiss Marjorie on the cheek, blowing Sarah a kiss at the same time.

Brigitte excused herself. "Sorry to leave this joyful reunion, but it's time I went to bed. You never know, I might even get an hour's sleep before I get called to someone falling off a barstool."

After they'd said goodnight and Bernard had suggested she might want to avoid a certain Dr Knott, Brigitte left the Jazz Bar, dragging the on-call bag behind her. Jason shuffled onto the bench next to Bernard.

"Have you been busy?" Sarah asked her fiancé.

"Non-stop. I've just left the boss and I'm still on duty, I'm afraid. He wants an update." Jason asked the waiter who appeared at the table for a sparkling mineral water. The rest of them opted for coffees, apart from Bernard, who asked for a pint of lager. Rachel was feeling a little lightheaded after her third Martini and lemonade of the evening.

"And here was I thinking you wanted to see your fiancée," Sarah teased.

Jason's adoring, though puffy, dark blue eyes sparkled back at her. "I always want to see you. Sorry for being impolite, I forgot to ask how you all are."

"It's a good job Brigitte's gone, or you'd get a lecture on the frailties of men," Bernard nudged Jason's arm. Jason laughed. They well knew Brigitte's opinions on the weaker sex, as she called men. Weaker, from her standpoint, meaning full of faults.

"Thankfully, we're more understanding," chimed in Marjorie. "Anyway, it is good to see you, Jason. I'd love to catch up on the wedding plans later in the cruise."

Jason blushed and looked at Sarah for help. She came to his rescue.

"We'll tell you all about it, but for now, Jason's busy."

"We've been busy, too, haven't we, Rachel?"

Rachel yawned, feeling the effects of more alcohol than she was used to. The drinks arrived and she took a large gulp of her coffee.

"Sorry, weariness catching up on me, too. Too many late nights." She looked at the dark lines under Jason's eyes. "You look as tired as I feel."

Jason stifled a yawn. "I was on the night shift last night, but I'll get to bed sometime tonight." He poured his sparkling water from the bottle into an ice-filled drinking glass before quickly scanning the surrounding area and lowering his voice. "Waverley said he told you your suspicions of atropine poisoning were confirmed."

"Yes, we met with him in Creams this afternoon. I guess it was too obvious not to be, on reflection. Is Waverley still gung-ho about keeping the cause of death quiet?"

"That wouldn't be the term I'd use, and he is having second thoughts about it. It's a big decision and not without risks. For now, though, we're continuing with routine enquiries – emphasis on routine – as we would about any sudden death on board. That at least paves the way for us to take it to the next level as and when the boss decides we need to. I've spoken to Leanne Bates, the wife of the deceased, Cody Spark, Demos Benedict," Rachel noticed the eye roll, "and another lady who's loosely connected called Krystal Brewer—"

"Oh? We haven't heard about her, is she one of the cast we've not yet seen?" Marjorie interrupted.

"No, not quite."

"Did you find out anything we should know?" Rachel asked.

"A few things. Mrs Bates doesn't seem to understand the meaning of the word bereaved. She goes on as if nothing's happened, which puts her at the top of the boss's suspect list."

"You sound as if you don't agree," suggested Sarah.

"Not sure. When I quizzed her as to why she didn't know how much insulin her husband had taken or what he'd eaten before his untimely death, she shrugged and told me he managed his own condition and that she was his wife, not his nurse. Mr Bates had priors for drugs misuse, so I asked whether she thought he might have been using before the show. She laughed and told me it was highly likely. But he also liked a drink. She gave me the stash of marijuana he'd brought on board after I told her if we found drugs, we would escort her off the ship to make her own way home. Not that we would have done so while she's a suspect in a murder inquiry, but she doesn't know that."

Marjorie frowned. "Silly man. Why do they do such idiotic things? And at his age, he should have known better."

"Yeah, that's true," Jason continued. "Then I tackled the rumour of his affair with Myra Slade." He took another gulp of his mineral water.

"And?" pressed Marjorie, impatiently.

"She tells me they had an 'open' marriage, and each saw other people when it suited. Myra was one of many. I went on to ask if she ever felt jealous and she was adamant she didn't. In fact, I'd say she couldn't care less. It doesn't appear they had an exclusive relationship, or that they took their marriage vows seriously."

Jason looked at Sarah and took her hand across the table. "I can't get my head around that sort of relationship, to be honest, but it could explain why she doesn't appear bothered about her husband's death – something she denies. She told me she cares deeply and just because she's not falling over with grief doesn't mean she's not grieving."

"As you said earlier, and from what I've observed, I don't think she is capable of such feelings," said Rachel. "I spoke to her, too. Your boss was right when he described her as icicles."

"Well, he has to be right about some things," quipped Marjorie. "I've certainly had my eyes opened since meeting Rachel here, but this is a new one on me. Were they what people refer to as swingers?"

Jason flushed. "Not quite. I think that's something different, but it could have been a part of their 'open' marriage."

"I didn't get very far with her at all," Rachel admitted. "I just seemed to wind her up, although when I asked about her relationship with the fictional Marvin Black, I think she was referring to her husband when she told me she had no love for him and that he was a drug addict and a waster. Obviously, I can't be certain because he was suitably cast as a washed-up rock star who also took drugs. I suspect they only stayed together for mutual advantage, most likely shared wealth. They'd invested heavily in Murder Mystery Creations; it wouldn't surprise me if Leanne was setting herself up for a takeover bid—"

"We can't deny she has motive, though," interrupted Marjorie. "Even if she didn't care about her husband's sleeping around, he may have got in the way of her ambition. Do you know how much she will inherit, Jason? Are there any children involved?"

"No children, and as yet we know little about their finances. We can only dig so far from this end. She doesn't have any criminal record, either."

"How did you find the beguiling Demos?" Marjorie asked. "Can you believe he flirted with me?"

Jason's fist clenched around his water glass and his face clouded. "He's a pathetic leech. According to my new friend Krystal Brewer, he's looking for an older woman to marry and fund his lifestyle. Stay away from him, Marjorie."

"You don't need to worry about me. I saw right through him from the moment we met, although I have to say it's quite flattering at my age to receive such attention from a handsome young man."

Marjorie's joke was wasted on Jason, who glared at his drink.

"I'm serious, Marjorie, and he could be dangerous."

"You don't think he's our killer, surely?"

"Why not? His only interest is money. What if Dudley Bates was a threat? Maybe his next target will be Leanne."

"But we don't know whether she's wealthy enough, you just said so yourself. Besides, Marjorie and I know where his attentions are focussed at present," Rachel said. "A woman called Enid. She and her daughter sit at our table and he chats to them. I think he's told them about Dudley's death. I take it he doesn't suspect murder?"

Jason frowned again. "Not from our conversation. He believes it was Dudley's drug habit and lack of self-care regarding his medical condition that caused his demise. No-one I spoke to seems to care one bit about the man's death. Demos had also told Krystal about the death, despite the fact that I warned him, when I spoke to him, not to go around telling people about it. He's got a loose tongue, and from what I hear, he's also a heavy drinker. Those two things combined don't give me much reassurance on the gossip front."

"I can confirm the heavy drinking as a first-hand witness," said Marjorie. "I suppose he told you Myra passed him over for promotion in favour of Dudley?"

"Really? How did he feel about that?" Jason asked, sitting upright.

"Angry, but the more he went on about it, and the more I think about it, the more he came across as just a 'woe is me' type of person. Rachel doesn't think the motive's strong enough, but who knows?"

"I'll let the boss know later. As you say, you just don't know. I'd like it to be him – men like him make me sick." Creases lined Jason's forehead as he contemplated Demos

Benedict. Rachel wondered if he reminded him of the man who'd stolen his ex.

"Okay. So who's Krystal?" she asked.

Jason's eyes sparkled and he lost the cloud as he spoke. "I met her because of a possible theft, but it turns out she was in the wrong room. However, she had met Dudley Bates and knows Benedict. Apparently, they share the same agent for TV advertising work. It turns out Gladys Knott muscled in on the part Creations had promised Krystal just a week or so before the cruise. Krystal had gone into a room, thinking it was Dr Knott's, planning to scare her off so she could get the part she feels she's owed." Jason leaned back and grinned towards Marjorie. "You'd like her; she's a feisty old bird."

"Jason Goodridge, don't let me hear you speak of women as birds – joking or not!" Sarah chastised.

"What about the 'old'?" chuckled Marjorie. "I suppose that's all right, is it?"

Sarah's face reddened. "No. I didn't mean—" she stopped as they all burst into laughter, realising they were teasing her. Bernard, who had been quiet throughout the conversation, couldn't resist chipping in with his own tease.

"You fell for that one, Nurse Bradshaw."

Now it was Rachel's turn to speak. The mood became serious again as she explained to Jason what she had discovered through her few conversations, and about

Gladys Knott feigning illness when she saw her son holding Myra Slade.

"The boss spoke to Ms Slade. He thinks she's in the clear—"

"Which means she's probably guilty," interrupted Marjorie.

Jason smiled. Rachel knew he was well aware of his boss's tendency to jump to the wrong conclusion, but he would never say so.

"I spoke to Cody, Gladys Knott's son," he added.

"Now, he is a pathetic young man, isn't he?" said Marjorie. Rachel resisted the temptation to tease her friend about her frequent use of the word 'young' when referring to adults in their forties and fifties. "Still tied to his mother's apron at his age. I wonder she allowed him to come on the cruise at all."

"Apparently she didn't want him to come, and he almost capitulated, but he says he's very fond of Myra," said Jason. "I don't think he's had many girlfriends."

"Why doesn't that surprise me?" Marjorie huffed.

"Anyway, in order to keep both women happy, he got his mother the part playing the duchess. He's not as daft as he acts and obviously knows how to get his own way sometimes. On the murder front, there's no motive. He knew about Myra's affair with Dudley Bates; she's been upfront with him about her past. The boss says Myra is genuinely in love with Cody Spark."

"Not that there's any spark in him," Marjorie chuckled. "Although it ties in with what Demos told me and Myra told Rachel. You're right, Demos has verbal diarrhoea when it comes to information. As part of his pity party, he was positively gleeful at the prospect that Myra is going to have her heart broken when Cody's formidable mother breaks up the relationship. He's bitter."

"Doesn't surprise me. According to Krystal, Myra's got a habit of reneging on promises when it suits her," Jason added. "Although she got that information from Benedict."

"I'm afraid he also told me about Dudley's death," Marjorie said.

Jason sighed. "We're going to have to act fast to solve this one before everyone knows about the unfortunate man's demise."

"And I met a woman whose husband suspects something is amiss," said Rachel. "It wouldn't surprise me if he has wangled news of the death out of Demos, too. I was going to tell Waverley. I'm worried the man might put himself in danger without realising."

"You didn't tell me about this," Marjorie complained.

"I kept forgetting because we were going through the suspect list." Rachel looked at Jason. "All I know is the man's first name is Jo-Jo – could be short for something else – and his wife is Celia May. He's an ex homicide cop from Florida. Celia May says he videoed last night's performance and told her there's something strange going on, and when I saw them tonight, she was videoing and he was taking multiple notes. He got on well with Gladys Knott, from what I saw; in fact, she seemed star-struck. Anyway, he's elderly and has a limp from a gunshot wound to his right knee. I'd hate something to happen to him if he's seeing this as some sort of challenge."

"So much for the cruise line believing a murder mystery event would provide a unique experience to keep passengers entertained for days! You know what Waverley will say?" Jason grimaced.

Rachel laughed. "Something about amateur night and people minding their own business."

"Speaking of the boss, I'd better go fill him in. Then I'm going to crash. See you guys tomorrow. Try to get through the day without adding to the body count, please."

Rachel wondered if Jason had the same feeling she did. *This killer has only just begun.*

Chapter 16

Waverley remained convinced Leanne Bates was the perpetrator. She had both motive and opportunity.

"We just need to narrow it down to the means," he said to Jason. "Her husband was into drugs, and she knew about it. Who's to say she didn't brush up on poisoning? It's easy enough to do nowadays. She also had access to the script and would be familiar with her husband's health problems. It's got to be her, Goodridge. We have to focus on her for now."

"What about Demos Benedict, sir? Lady Marjorie says he resented not getting the assistant manager's job because Ms Slade went back on her word. He could have thought he'd be in with a chance of promotion again with Bates out of the way."

"The trouble is, it's a weak motive over some two-bit job opportunity that probably wouldn't pay that well, isn't it?"

"With him, it's all about the kudos he'd be able to present to the world. Or more importantly, his female fan club." Jason scowled, remembering what Krystal had told him about Benedict preying on rich women.

"Okay. Why don't you meet up with the Brewer woman again and find out what else she can tell you about the man? As far as I can tell from what we've found out – and it appears Rachel and Lady Marjorie concur – none of the others are in the frame. It's either Mrs Bates or Demos Benedict, until proven otherwise."

Jason looked at the notes on his tablet. "I don't remember you mentioning Nellie Hurst earlier, and neither Rachel nor Lady Marjorie got to speak to her."

"Mm, hang on, let me check." Waverley pulled a notebook from his pocket. He didn't use tablets – didn't trust them, he said – only a notebook or PC on his desk. "Ah yes. She's Myra's cousin. They're not close, but she's Myra's next of kin on paper, although she's older so unlikely to inherit." He read from his notes. "Made no secret of disapproving of Dudley Bates's relationship with Myra, but then, who would approve? I quite liked her: a straight talker, no messing, a bit harsh and doesn't like Leanne, I've written here. I asked what she thought would happen to the business if Cody married her cousin and she laughed, saying his mother would see to it there was no marriage."

"She could have been worried Myra might get back with Bates, though," Jason postulated.

"Not likely, and even if she did, it wouldn't affect her job. As I said, she's older and is unlikely to inherit if things go according to the natural way of things. Nellie told me quite openly she didn't really like Bates and the relationship had been a mistake. If it had been Myra who was killed, we'd be inundated with suspects, but it wasn't. You've seen the background checks, I take it?"

"Yes, sir. Nothing comes up for Nellie. History of being a sought-after actress in her twenties, out of work when she hit fifty and working for her cousin since the Murder Mystery Creations started. If Myra wasn't such a cutthroat businesswoman, I'd feel sorry for her for falling in love with a man down on his luck with a domineering mother."

"You're referring to the tragic death of his fiancée, I take it?"

Jason nodded; he didn't know how he'd go on without Sarah in his life. Best not to think about it. "I wonder if that's why his mother is so protective. She can't have always been like that; she's been married twice herself and had a successful career in medicine."

"Maybe, or perhaps she has more time on her hands now she's on her own and retired. No-one wants to be lonely in old age. I've been there; before I met Brenda, I..."

Jason waited, but Waverley would not continue. He knew the boss's first wife had gone off with his friend and it had devastated him, according to Sarah. Waverley was now married to a head baker on board the *Coral*, Brenda, and they were good together, as Waverley's ever-expanding waistline showed.

Jason grinned. *I'd take that for a happy marriage.*

"Do you mind if I call it a night, sir? I'm beat."

"Of course. Once you've spoken to Mrs Brewer tomorrow, we should be able to think about an arrest. It'll be down to the UK police to check the Bates' home to find out what Mrs Bates was up to."

Jason couldn't push aside the nagging doubt he had over Leanne Bates's guilt. He'd spoken to her. She was cold, yes, but she made no attempt at pretending to be the heartbroken widow. Surely a killer would at least try? And she was an actress, so she'd be able to pull it off. Unless the boss was right: she didn't know they knew the death was murder.

He rubbed his head. He was torn between going straight to bed or nipping to the crew dining room below decks for a snack. His stomach groaning made the decision for him.

He regretted it as soon as he walked into the crew bar he had to pass through to get to the dining room. The crew came here to let their hair down; it was late and many of them were sloshed. A few of the men from engineering gave him a nod; others gave him a wide berth. He didn't come down here often, and when he did, it was usually to break up a fight or deal with some company rule infringement or other.

He walked straight up to the bar and asked for a sparkling mineral water before heading on through to the crew dining room. Collecting a plate of fish and chips, he found a seat when a mixed-sex group moved out of his way. He smiled, then slapped himself on the head.

I forgot to tell the boss about the man Rachel was worried about. Wondering whether he should do so now, he decided the boss needed downtime too, and anyway, he already had an arrest in his sights. The killer wouldn't be so stupid as to kill again tonight, especially not a passenger.

Jason saw Maria, Krystal's stateroom attendant, at a nearby table with a group of Filipino friends, having supper. He smiled.

"Good evening, sir. We don't see you down here very often."

"Just grabbing a bite to eat. How's Mrs Brewer?"

"She's fine, although David told me he saw her on deck nine again, this time with a suave-looking gentleman. An actor, he said."

"When was this?"

"A couple of hours ago."

"Has David gone to bed?"

"No, sir, he's through there, playing cards with his mates."

Jason gobbled up his food and drained his glass before returning to the crew bar. He asked the barman where David was, and the guy reluctantly pointed to a table in the far corner. Obviously some gambling was going on, but Jason wasn't interested in that. He held his hand up when he approached as the men shuffled money off the table.

"Evening, guys. Do you mind if I have a quick word with David, and then I'll leave you to your friendly game of poker?"

Audible sighs of relief spread around the table, but David's eyes widened. "Have I done something wrong?"

"Not at all. I just wanted to know if you saw Mrs Brewer this evening, the woman who was in the couple's room last night?"

"Yes, sir, but she was nowhere near their room. She was down the other end of the corridor with a man."

"Did she see you?"

"No, sir."

"What did the man look like?"

"Around forty, beard, moustache, good-looking. He's one of the actors from the Murder Mystery Creations. They have rooms on deck nine, but I don't see to them. They should be downstairs."

Jason knew that the cruise line usually put entertainment employees in shared rooms at or below the waterline, but Myra Blade had negotiated staterooms as part of the contract.

"What room is the gentleman in?"

"Sorry, sir. I don't know. Is anything wrong?"

"Nothing, I just want to make sure our Mrs Brewer isn't straying into other guests' rooms again, that's all."

"No, sir. She and the gentleman were having an intense discussion about something, but I heard her laugh before she went into his room."

"Thank you, David. I'll leave you to get back to your game."

It was too late to try contacting Krystal now; he'd speak to her in the morning to find out more about Demos Benedict and what gossip she'd managed to get out of him.

Chapter 17

The vision of an elderly man lying dead at the bottom of a set of stairs startled Rachel from her sleep. Trying to shake off the feeling that Jo-Jo was in danger, she turned over and pulled the pillow over her head. It was no use. Sleep had deserted her.

She looked at the time: 5am. She leapt out of bed, thankful that generally she was a morning person, and made herself a coffee. Opening the curtains, she stared into the darkness, wondering how Scandinavians coped with the brief daylight hours from autumn through to spring. It was bad enough in England, but here the nights were so much longer.

The ship was docking silently in the dark while most people slept. Stavanger, a city in southern Norway, was their first stop.

Rachel stayed on the balcony for a while, listening to the activity on the dockside while enjoying her coffee. Her balcony was at the rear of the ship on the starboard side, so she couldn't see the dockside. The moon was bright in the sky and its light reflected off the otherwise dark sea behind her.

The ship came to a halt, and she heard a ping coming from the corridor outside as the captain announced they had docked. An hour and a half had passed since she got up. She grabbed her phone and saw she had a signal. She dialled.

Carlos answered immediately. "I was hoping you'd call early. How's the trip?"

"It's interesting so far." Rachel deliberated whether to mention the dead body. "You'll never believe what activity Marjorie booked us on to."

"Jet skiing, horse riding, Segway, cartwheels?" Carlos laughed. "Or perhaps being more realistic, a luxury spa for two?"

"I wish! I'd even take the jet skiing. Nope, she booked us a five-night murder mystery called 'Murder on Deck'."

"Nooooo! Now that I would not have guessed. Couldn't you refuse?"

"Have you ever tried refusing Marjorie anything? Anyway, the whole thing must have cost a fortune. We've taken over the Cocktail Lounge for five nights, all drinks included, five course dinners and a murder mystery company headed up by a Meryl Streep lookalike putting on nightly shows."

Carlos laughed loudly. "Never a dull moment when Marjorie's around. I'm sorry I'm not there. Lady and I miss you."

"And I miss you. How's work?"

"Not great. I've got to travel up to Edinburgh today. Another reason I hoped you'd call early."

"Will you be taking the train?"

"No, I'm driving. The client's in Keswick, but the missing person was last seen in Edinburgh."

"Why you?"

"A friend of a friend. You know how these things work. They haven't heard from their daughter for over a week other than by text. They're convinced something's happened to her. The police think she's just taking some time out of university."

Rachel's brain processed the many possibilities facing the police. "If they've received texts, why are they worried?"

"They say she never texts them. She always phones. And the last text told them she was going away for a break and would be out of a signal area for a fortnight. She might well have met some fella she doesn't want to mention, but my friend says the parents are not the overreacting types, so I'm meeting them later today before trying to track her down."

"I hope it is just a blip and she has gone for a break. Text me when you get to Edinburgh. We have stops for the next four days so we can talk anytime."

"Thanks, Rachel. I'm going to head into the office early to finish up a report, and then Lady and I will head north. What are you doing today?"

"We've decided to take the hop-on, hop-off bus. Sarah and Jason are working, but they're joining us tomorrow for a trip when we get to Nordfjordeid."

"You've been practising how to say that, haven't you?" He laughed again. "I've got your itinerary so I know exactly where you are, my darling. Enjoy your day out. I love you."

"I love you too, Carlos. Drive carefully, won't you?"

"I will."

"Give Lady a big hug and a treat from me."

"I'll give her the hug. She gets far too many treats. Ciao for now."

"Ciao, Carlos." Rachel pressed the call end button, wishing she'd used video call rather than audio. She told herself she'd not had the opportunity to mention the death of Dudley Bates, rather than been deliberately keeping it from him.

It sounds like he has enough to deal with without worrying about me being embroiled in yet another murder. I'll tell him later.

After taking a shower and ordering a fresh pot of coffee from the kitchen, she tried to fight off the feeling that there was more to this murder than she was seeing. Marjorie remained convinced the perpetrator was either Myra Slade or Leanne Bates. To Rachel, Leanne Bates seemed the obvious choice, with Demos Benedict a close second. *Sometimes, the most obvious people are the ones.*

One thing was certain: it was a well-planned crime rather than an opportunistic one. Whoever killed Dudley knew about his health condition, his tendency to self-neglect and his drug habit. On top of that, they knew the script and that it involved the fictional use of Deadly Nightshade to kill the victim, who just happened to be played by Dudley Bates.

Something else niggled away at the back of her mind, something that was just out of reach for the moment. She wished she had access to footage from the performance on the night Dudley had been killed.

Of course, you idiot. You need to track down Jo-Jo and ask to look at the recording he took.

Dismissing her earlier concerns about him being in danger, she called Marjorie's room and told her she'd spoken to Carlos and what he was doing today.

"I do hope the young woman is all right. I don't like the cases your husband is getting wrapped up in these days. It was all well and good being a private investigator when he was tracking down harmless criminals—"

"There's no such thing as a harmless criminal, but I know what you mean." Rachel moved the topic on to Jo-Jo and told Marjorie what she planned to do.

"But won't he find it odd? I thought you wanted him to stay out of the investigation."

"I do, but I'm sure we can come up with some excuse. Let's think about it."

***

Rachel and Marjorie returned to the *Coral Queen* at 3pm after their tour of Stavanger. Although it was Rachel's first visit to the Norwegian Fjords, her older friend had been many times before.

As they boarded, Rachel spotted Waverley overseeing security.

"Is this an ominous sign?" whispered Marjorie.

"Not necessarily. He does sometimes train new recruits. Also, there's usually more than one case on the go for the security team. I took a visit into the hot den behind their security operations once, and it was like being in a police briefing room."

Marjorie raised an eyebrow. "I hadn't considered that, but Jason mentions other cases from time to time, doesn't he?"

After they'd passed through security, Waverley nodded a greeting. "Good afternoon, ladies. Nice day?"

"Very pleasant, thank you," replied Marjorie.

Waverley said nothing else and they boarded without incident.

"Obviously not us he's waiting for, if he is waiting for someone," Rachel said.

"I'm pleased, to be honest. I'm rather tired. Would you mind if I go for a lie down before the cocktail party?"

"Of course not. Are you feeling all right? I'm sorry if I walked you too far."

"Don't fuss, dear. People of my age need the occasional rest, that's all. I enjoyed the walking, although I may have overdone it a little."

"I'll see you to your room before I meet Sarah in Creams."

"You'll do no such thing. Off you go. You run up the stairs and burn some energy off. I know you want to."

Rachel laughed. "You're right. I need some exercise; I didn't get my early morning run after chatting to Carlos, but it was worth the sacrifice."

The lift arrived and Marjorie got in. *Is it my imagination or does she seem frailer since her bout of pneumonia?* Unable to bear the idea that Marjorie might be anything other than a strong octogenarian, Rachel followed her friend's suggestion and ran up the stairs to deck four where Creams was situated. It was only two floors up. Sarah was already there, and Rachel was pleased to see there were no other members of the medical team with her. It would give them a proper chance to catch up.

"Hi, Rachel. I know we didn't arrange to meet, but I thought I'd pop in here just in case. Where's Marjorie?"

"Gone for a lie down; I think I wore her out. I sometimes forget how old she is, she's so sharp mentally."

"Which is just how she likes it. She wouldn't want you fussing over her like she's going to snap at any moment."

"More or less what she told me when I offered to see her back to her room."

"There you are, then. I don't think this murder business helps," Sarah lowered her voice. "I really don't think she expected to be tracking down another murderer on this voyage, no matter what she says or how much she pretends she's enjoying it."

"You could be right there. Maybe I should step back and tell Waverley to get on with it. I'm not relishing it either."

"You'll get no argument from me if you do. It'll be the most sensible decision you've made for ages – apart from marrying Carlos, of course." Sarah chuckled.

They ordered tea and Rachel's favourite cinnamon whirls. She was pleased Creams was relatively quiet. Port days gave the crew time to unwind even if they were on duty; apart from a minority of passengers who never got off the ship, most people went ashore to enjoy excursions and terra firma.

"I spoke to Carlos this morning. He's off to Edinburgh. Could even be there by now."

Sarah's eyebrows rose. "Work, I presume?"

Rachel explained about the possible missing person case her husband had been asked to investigate. "He was stopping off in the Lake District to speak to the girl's parents en route."

"Would it be awful if I said I hope the girl has done something out of character, like taking off on her own or with a group of friends?"

"I'm hoping the same thing. Carlos said that's what the police think has happened, especially considering text messages sent from her phone."

Their drinks and pastries arrived, and they enjoyed the comfortable silence that only good friends can share. Then Rachel's mind wandered back to Marjorie.

"You seem worried. Is it about the case you're supposedly going to withdraw from?" Sarah giggled.

"I was thinking about Marjorie, actually. I noticed for the first time just before I came to meet you how pasty she looks after that dreadful pneumonia episode."

"Don't worry too much. Pneumonia can knock the stuffing out of elderly people – and young ones, for that matter – but she's otherwise fit and healthy. She seemed fine last night. Remember, you're both having late nights and early mornings. I can't keep up with you sometimes, Rachel, and I'm the same age."

Rachel smiled. "You're right. I'll go a bit slower and suggest to Marjorie we pack in the investigation. I might even suggest we cut and run from 'Murder on Deck' altogether, then we won't be tempted to change our minds."

"I hope you're serious, Rachel, because there's nothing I'd like more. Waverley has this habit of telling you not to investigate one minute, and then putting you on the frontline the next. Jason thinks he's having second thoughts about keeping the murder a secret, anyway, so I expect he'll be pleased to get on with it. And from what we heard about Demos Benedict's untethered mouth last night, he's going to tell everyone he meets that Dudley's dead. With passengers being hyped up to investigate a fictional murder, it won't take long for some of them to work out what really happened. Just like you did."

"I expect the murderer didn't account for Demos and his big mouth," agreed Rachel. "Last night I was convinced Dudley's murder was the first of many. It makes little sense."

Sarah's jaw dropped. "Why on earth would you think that?"

"I have no idea. Gut feeling."

Sarah cupped her head in her hands. "You and your gut feelings. You get out of there while you still can. No excuses, Rachel Jacobi-Prince! Leave it be, and I hope to God you're wrong."

But Rachel had finally said out loud what she'd been thinking and was more convinced than ever it was true.

Chapter 18

Rachel stood outside Marjorie's room, determined to persuade her to do the right thing and back away from the investigation. *What was I thinking agreeing to Waverley's crazy plan, anyway? It's fine when it's just me, but I will not put Marjorie's health at risk.* The whole idea of an autumn cruise had been to help with her elderly friend's convalescence.

Not for the first time, Rachel wished Marjorie hadn't booked the surprise murder mystery event. She knocked, but there was no reply. She was about to head back to her room to phone when she saw Mario.

"Mario, could you open Lady Marjorie's door? She went for a nap a while ago, but I think she needs to wake up and get ready for dinner now."

"Of course Miss… Mrs Rachel." He swiped his key in the door. "I'll go and get you some fresh tea. I know how much Lady Marjorie likes her tea."

"Thanks, Mario." Rachel opened the door and walked straight through into Marjorie's bedroom. It was dark, but she saw the shadow. Her friend was lying in a heap next to the bed.

Rachel rushed back and opened the door to the corridor. "Mario, get help! Call a doctor." She then flicked the light switch and ran back into the bedroom to check on her friend. Marjorie's pulse was weak and thready; her eyes flickered and she groaned. Rachel knelt on a wet patch on the carpet and saw an empty glass.

"Stay with me, Marjorie. Please, please, stay with me." Rachel lifted her friend's head and cradled her in her arms. "I'm so sorry, I should have stayed with you."

Dr Bentley was the first to arrive, followed immediately by Gwen. Rachel lifted her head to look at them, tears flowing unashamedly down her face.

"Please, save her."

Dr Bentley checked Marjorie's vitals in a flash.

"Were you here when she collapsed?" asked Gwen.

"No, she went for a lie down after our tour. She must have woken, tried to have a drink of water and fell."

"Open the curtains and the balcony doors, she feels hot as hell," suggested Dr Bentley.

Once Rachel had pulled the heavy drapes and opened the doors, she returned to where Dr Bentley and Gwen were assessing her friend. The redness on Marjorie's face was obvious.

"What is it?" Rachel asked.

Dr Bentley stared at Gwen with disbelief. "Atropine?"

Gwen spoke into her radio and summoned help.

Bernard and Janet Plover arrived with a stretcher, and they carefully transferred Marjorie onto it. It delighted Rachel to hear another groan coming from her, and by the time they got to the lift, Marjorie opened her eyes.

"What happened?"

"I think someone tried to poison you is what happened," snapped Dr Bentley. "I do wish you and Rachel here would stay out of trouble. Waverley's going to get an earful when I see him."

"You won't need to wait long," said Gwen. "I called him from Marjorie's room while you were getting her on the trolley. I told him to bag up the water bottle and glass while he's at it. We can drop it into the nearest path lab tomorrow."

"Good thinking, Gwen."

"I spat most of it out," mumbled Marjorie. "Tasted dreadful."

"That action probably saved your life. I'm surprised you drank any of it," Dr Bentley said.

"Didn't it taste bitter?" Rachel quizzed.

"Yes, horrible. I felt the effects almost as soon as I swallowed."

"Whoever did this might have used a lower dose for someone of Marjorie's age," said Dr Bentley. "If I'm honest, I'm amazed you survived."

The doctors were talking about the plan of action as they wheeled Marjorie into the infirmary.

"Pilocarpine," Marjorie said weakly. "I have glaucoma in my left eye. I expect the eye drops protected me."

"That explains it," said Janet.

"I still think you've been interfering where you shouldn't and our security chief should have more sense. Now, let's get you into bed. You're staying here until you're fully recovered, and I forbid you to go anywhere near this killer again." Dr Bentley's sharp tone showed his fondness for Marjorie, and she and Rachel understood.

"Well, if I knew who that was, I'd do as you instruct, Dr Bentley." Marjorie winked at Rachel, whose relief knew no bounds.

After Marjorie had been settled into a bed on the ward and the medics had assured Rachel her friend would make a full recovery, she relaxed for the first time since finding her.

"Where did the water come from?"

"My room," replied Marjorie. "That's what's so odd. Mario must have put it there. He knows I like a bottle at room temperature. Sometimes when it's too cold, it gives me the shivers."

"There has to be some other explanation. Had someone opened it?"

"I don't remember; I don't think so. It's usually a fresh bottle."

Rachel didn't ask anything else, as Marjorie looked tired. The doctors had departed along with Gwen, leaving Bernard in charge of the patient. Rachel popped out to Gwen's office for reassurance that Marjorie really would make a full recovery.

"Absolutely, Rachel. I agree with Graham, though. She shouldn't put herself at risk anymore. Waverley will be here soon and I'm sure he'll be gutted at what's happened. Especially after the ear bashing I heard Graham give him before he went into surgery."

Rachel almost felt sorry for Waverley, but she was also annoyed with him, and herself, over what had happened. "Thanks, Gwen. I'll get back to the infirmary."

A few minutes later, Sarah popped in to check on them both. Marjorie fell asleep shortly afterwards. Rachel glanced at the monitors to make sure everything was as it should be. She was no expert, but she knew what a normal pulse, blood pressure and oxygen saturation was.

"I guess this means you won't let it drop even if you're told to now," Sarah said.

Rachel gritted her teeth. "You're so right. Nothing is going to stop me from finding out who did this. It just got personal."

"Graham told me he thinks it was a lower dose than the one given to Dudley Bates. Perhaps whoever did it was trying to scare her or both of you off."

"Well, it hasn't worked. Just the opposite, in fact. I'll hunt them down and make sure we put them behind bars for a very long time. We don't know if it was a lower dose anyway because Marjorie spat it out, and they seem to think her eye drops helped reverse its effect."

"Yes, pilocarpine's an antidote for atropine."

Marjorie opened her eyes. "Are you still here, Rachel? You need to get to the Cocktail Lounge and find our killer. If anyone asks, perhaps you should tell them I'm dead." Marjorie's colour had returned to normal, but she still looked frail.

"It wouldn't work. They'd wonder – quite rightly – why I was at the party. I'll tell them you took ill and were taken to the hospital in Stavanger, but I needed to come back to the ship to stay with our things, or something like that. I don't want anyone knowing you're still aboard for now."

Marjorie sat up straight. "Well, if I'm not dead, I hope you don't think I'm going to hide away like some mouse, because I'm not. I'll be out of here tomorrow and no-one is going to stop me."

"Fine," snapped Rachel. "You can be 'discharged' from hospital tomorrow and rejoin the ship." She softened. "Sorry, I don't mean to snap, but I was really worried. I thought you were going to die, Marjorie."

Marjorie took her hand. "Well, I didn't. It'll take more than a bit of cheap poison to get rid of me. Now, go on and investigate. I'll be all right. Bernard over there has threatened to beat me at chess, which should be entertaining."

"He is quite good," Sarah said.

"So am I, dear. So am I."

Rachel kissed Marjorie on the cheek and walked out of the infirmary with Sarah. She heard Waverley's voice coming from Gwen's room.

"I think he's waiting for you," whispered Sarah.

"I'm sure he is, but I've got things to do. Don't tell him I've left until you have to. I need to rush upstairs and change for dinner. Someone is going to answer for this."

***

Rachel changed from casual clothes into a cocktail dress for the evening. The only remaining sign that she'd found Marjorie so close to death was her shaking hands. Fear of how different things could have been if Marjorie had swallowed more of the atropine threatened to overwhelm her. She shook her head to dispel such morose notions from her brain.

Before leaving, she called down to the infirmary.

"We're fine," Bernard answered. "The old girl's well enough to keep beating me at chess. Things are getting better, though: I've just won a game. Here, have a word."

Marjorie came on the line, but not before Rachel heard her rebuke Bernard for calling her an old girl. They both giggled in the background.

"Don't you worry about me, Rachel. I'm going to teach this young man how to lose gracefully," she chuckled. "Be careful tonight, won't you? Oh, and be on the lookout. His

Lordship is looking for you. He's decided it's time to hand it over to the professionals."

Rachel huffed. "He should have thought of that before someone poisoned you."

"Do you have any ideas on who it could have been? I'm ruling out that young man, Demos; he's far too interested in my money to contemplate such a thing. I don't think I spoke to anyone else, other than when you and I had a word with the Spark fellow."

Rachel pressed hard on her forehead. She had been racking her brains, trying to narrow the suspects down to one person.

"It has to be someone you spoke to."

"It's not Demos, Rachel."

"We'll see, as you say. He's the only one of the main cast you interviewed. It wouldn't be Cody; he saves lives for a living, albeit animal ones."

"I don't see it being Demos. As I said already," Marjorie sighed, "he'd be too interested in my money and how I might help further his career to want me out of the way. Unless he really did kill Dudley Bates out of jealousy."

"It's all a bit of a mess, isn't it? I do want to speak to Demos tonight, though. Perhaps he told someone about you asking questions. You didn't tell him we were investigating the murder, did you?"

"I didn't get to ask him very much at all, to be honest, his conversation comprising me, me, me. The only investigation I referred to was that of the pretend murder of Marvin Black. Just as he told me the man had died for real, they summoned him backstage and me to dinner. I can't remember saying anything else, but I may have done. He was plying me with drink; I felt slightly woozy."

"Right. Well, he's my starting point."

"Have you spoken to Mario about the water?"

"Not yet. I can't get hold of him; an unfamiliar man is covering who won't tell me where he is. I suspect Waverley's summoned him for an explanation."

"As long as the blundering idiot hasn't arrested him."

Rachel hoped the same. "I don't think he will. There will be a reasonable explanation as to how the bottle got into your room. Mario is harmless as a fly and adores you."

"Right. Well, Nurse Guinto here has just set up our next game, so you go catch our killer. But promise me you'll be careful."

"I promise."

Rachel checked the time and realised she was running late if she wanted to question Demos before dinner. She grabbed an evening bag from the bed and placed her cruise and room card inside before dashing out.

There were fewer people in the Cocktail Lounge tonight; perhaps some were tired after the day ashore. She scanned the room in search of the loose-lipped Demos Benedict. *I can't think why he reminded me of Carlos, he's nothing like him.* When she spotted him surrounded by cooing women, including Enid and Kate, she headed in his direction. No-one was going to stop her getting near him tonight, and it wasn't his charm drawing her.

A few feet out, someone blocked her path. It was the man called Jo-Jo.

"Pardon me, mam. The steely flint in your eyes tells me you're heading for trouble."

Rachel stared down at the unassuming man whose wife she had spoken to last night. "I'm sorry, I'm in a hurry. Please excuse me."

"Not before you tell me what you're up to. My wife told me about you, and I don't believe the questions you asked were those of someone interested in a fictional murder."

As even more women were flocking round Demos, Rachel decided now might not be the time to barge in without making a scene. Although she felt very much like making a scene, it wouldn't be in the best interests of her investigation. Realising she was still fuming about the attempt on Marjorie's life, she recognised the need to take a moment and become more objective.

Throwing one last glare towards Demos, she looked down at the white-haired man with the piercing green eyes once more. "Your wife told me you were a police officer before you… erm… retired."

"Yep. Took one for the team." He tapped his knee with his walking stick. "Jo-Jo Falconi at your service. Why don't we take a seat?" Jo-Jo nodded towards the quiet bar. Most passengers were milling around in groups, chatting among themselves or quizzing the Creations cast.

"Rachel Jacobi-Prince." She leaned down and whispered, "Detective Sergeant Rachel Prince; I use my maiden name for work."

The older man's eyes twinkled. "I thought as much. Not much of a holiday, something like this, for a serving cop."

"You're telling me; it was my friend's idea."

"The elderly woman you sit with for dinner? I take it the two other women are with you too?"

"How astute you are, Mr Falconi."

"Jo-Jo, please."

"Okay, Jo-Jo. No, we only met the other two on the first night; they're fans of his." Rachel glared again in Demos's direction.

"Where is your friend tonight?"

"She's resting. I think I exhausted her on our day out."

"We took one of the coach tours; unfortunately, I can't walk so far these days. Damn knee gives me gyp." Jo-Jo hit his knee with a stick.

"I'm not surprised if you hit it like that," Rachel laughed. She liked this man and sensed his shrewd eyes had picked up more than he was letting on. "Where's Celia May? I don't think I've seen her."

"She's been doing the rounds, interviewing. I sound too much like a cop when I do it. She's just caught up with Demos Benedict, the man you were about to interrogate; they're over there." He pointed towards the crowd of women waiting to speak to Demos. Celia May was holding her ground, quizzing him with notebook in hand. "He's the hunk who likes to take women for a ride. Mind you, if I had his looks, I might be tempted." Jo-Jo laughed, a deep, guttural sound.

"I'd like to think you wouldn't," Rachel joined in his laughter.

"I'm surprised he's not made a play for you; you're a beauty, I must say."

Rachel felt her cheeks redden, but took the compliment as well-meant. "As I said, I'm married. Besides, I don't think I'm rich enough for Mr Benedict. He has made a play – as you put it – for my friend, though. Not to mention the two women we dine with, who are both infatuated."

"Beguiled, more like," Jo-Jo scowled at the man. "He's up to no good, of that I'm certain. What's your interest in him? The look in your eyes when I intercepted you tells me it's got nothing to do with this fictional claptrap."

Rachel didn't get the opportunity to answer. The punctual call for dinner ended their conversation.

Jo-Jo shrugged. "Better take my place. I'd like to speak with you again, Rachel. Perhaps we could trade notes. Catch you later."

Rachel would have liked to find out his thoughts on the death of Dudley Bates, and to warn him to be careful. She would make sure to do so later.

Chapter 19

Rachel tried hard to concentrate on the evening's performance, but her head was spinning. The tension on stage, though, was palpable and brought her back into the room. Each person pointed the finger at others until all of them had a motive for committing the murder. Petty bickering, the result of years of concealed bitterness, surfaced through clever scriptwriting as the act went on.

Myra Slade was playing a part tonight as the ship's doctor, who was assisting the chief security officer with his enquiries into who might have had access to and knowledge of the Deadly Nightshade plant. *Good point,* thought Rachel as she studied the cast.

Gladys Knott's performance as the all-powerful duchess grew as the tension heightened. Her insults at the incompetence of Myra as the ship's doctor appeared to Rachel at times to be off-script, judging by Myra's reaction.

The two women sparred back and forth, much to the amusement of the duchess's grandson, Sly Toner, played by Demos, and her sister, played by Leanne Bates.

Rachel studied each cast member in turn and couldn't help feeling the boundary between fact and fiction was blurring. The barman, aka Cody Spark, was torn between one and the other during a scene when both women asked him for a drink at once. It was almost comical, and in the end – like in the real world – the duchess won the fight for his attention.

By the end of the show, all suspicion had fallen onto the lounge singer Toni Cleeves, played by Nellie Hurst, as it transpired she was being blackmailed by Marvin Black over an affair she had had with the duchess's late husband. As on previous nights, enthusiastic applause sounded throughout the Cocktail Lounge after the curtains closed. When they opened for the bows, Myra Slade, well deserving of her nickname 'Blade' tonight, seemingly couldn't resist a deathly glare at the duchess's back while the older woman took a bow at the front as the star of this evening's show. A pattern was developing where one person played a greater part during each act. Gladys Knott was revelling in hers, taking far too long to return to the line for the whole-cast bows.

After the customary three ovations, the curtains closed for the last time. Enid and Kate were still clapping while Rachel finished a glass of water. She was staying on the wagon tonight, determined to keep her focus.

"Bravo," Enid shouted before taking her seat. Neither of the women had shown much interest when Rachel told them Marjorie was sitting out this evening's performance, but now Enid looked at her.

"It's a shame your friend wasn't here to see the show. Such a wonderful performance. The duchess was mesmerising tonight, wasn't she?"

"Not as mesmerising as Demos, Mum."

"It was a good show," said Rachel, not that interested in committing to the Demos admiration society.

"Yes," Kate went on. "It is a shame your friend—"

"Marjorie," said Rachel, wondering why neither woman was using Marjorie's name when they had been so friendly on previous evenings.

"Yes, Marjorie. What a shame she didn't see Demos tonight. She never said she had contacts in show business." Kate's eyes narrowed into thin lines, barely showing their light green colour. "Demos told us she might help him find another job."

Rachel clicked as to the reason why Kate in particular had been slightly offhand during dinner. Locking eyes with the woman, she understood where the expression 'green with envy' came from. A sudden thought occurred to her, but she reined it in for a moment.

"Marjorie has a lot of contacts. She told me Demos had been upset, bemoaning how he had been passed over for Dudley Bates as assistant manager. She's a good listener, that's all."

"As long as she's not stringing him along," Kate snapped.

"What are you implying?"

Enid tried intervening. "Kate, I'm sure Marjorie was just trying to be helpful."

Kate pouted. "As long as she's not trying to lure him in. A lot of women do that to him, you know."

"That's absurd!" Rachel was spoiling for a fight, and she could read from Kate's body language that she was, too. Taking deep breaths learned through her lifelong love of the karate discipline, Rachel toned her temper down. "As your mother said, Marjorie was just trying to help a man she thought had been wronged. Don't worry, I'll let her know she was mistaken and that Demos doesn't need her help."

Enid's eyes widened. "Please don't do that. Kate meant nothing; it's just she and Demos have hit it off and she doesn't want to see him hurt."

"When did Demos tell you about their conversation, anyway? Marjorie didn't mention it to me until this evening when I left for dinner." Rachel had changed her mind about the hospital story, but now wished she'd stuck with it. She would not let Marjorie out of her sight.

"He told us last night after the show," said Enid. "He was very excited about it, and so are we, aren't we, Kate? It would be far better for Demos if he does what makes him happy."

The difference between a mother's love, a sacrificial one, and Kate's love, a selfish one, couldn't have been clearer if Rachel had been listening to one of her father's sermons. Brendan Prince was a vicar and one of his favourite topics was that of a mother's love.

"I wouldn't want him to leave the Creations. The weekends wouldn't be the same without him." Kate's sullenness turned her plain face into that of one of the wicked sisters in the Cinderella story.

Rachel had given Demos Benedict enough airtime. "So who do you think killed Dudley?" she asked.

Both women were taken aback. Enid's face turned ashen, and Rachel wondered if the older woman had the same suspicion she herself now entertained.

"You mean Marvin Black?"

"Whoops! Yes, that's who I meant. But Demos told Marjorie the actor playing him, Dudley Bates, also died after the show on the first night. Didn't he tell you?"

"Of course he told us," snapped Kate. "He told us not to tell anyone."

Rachel smirked inwardly at Demos telling people not to say something that he was spreading around like butter. Not wanting to provoke Kate any further in case she stormed off, she murmured, "I thought he was quite close to you both, so imagined he would have taken you into his confidence. You don't think Dudley Bates was actually murdered, do you?"

With the bombshell delivered, Rachel keenly watched each woman's reaction, in particular Kate's.

Enid laughed nervously. "I don't think we should make light of a man's death, Rachel."

Kate opened and closed her mouth a few times, reminding Rachel of a goldfish. "Demos says he was diabetic and died from complications."

"All the same," Rachel persisted, "his act was so realistic, it makes me wonder if he really was poisoned."

Enid's light brown eyes darted nervously from Kate to Rachel and back again. "I don't think I can contemplate anyone being murdered in real life. Please don't take it all so seriously, it was just an unfortunate coincidence. Apparently, Dudley's health wasn't the best. The Murder Mystery Creations actors are extremely talented and professional, and as this is your first experience, I fear you might be letting your imagination run amok."

Then why do you suspect your daughter had something to do with Dudley's death? Rachel was tempted to retort, but she didn't want to alienate them now she was closing in.

"You're probably right. Marjorie's always telling me I have a vivid imagination. It seems unlikely anyone would be so bold as to kill someone in front of a packed audience. Still—"

Enid exhaled and took her daughter's hand. "It's time we went to bed. We've had a long day."

"I forgot to ask where you went today?" Rachel stared straight at Kate.

"Mum went on a coach trip. I had a headache, so stayed on board."

Rachel forced herself not to react. "Shame you missed the sights. Still, I expect you found something to keep you occupied." She didn't let up her eye lock for one moment.

"As a matter of fact, I did." Kate's malicious glare mocked Rachel's challenging one.

Enid appeared baffled and pulled Kate's arm. "Come on, Kate. Goodnight, Rachel. We look forward to seeing Marjorie again tomorrow."

Kate reluctantly rose from her chair, scraping it on the floor in her anger. Rachel had certainly forced a reaction and added a new suspect to her list. The only problem was Kate didn't have access to the stage when Dudley died. She needed time to think it through, but first she wanted to check Marjorie was okay before going to see Waverley.

She had hoped to catch Jo-Jo after the show, but Kate's, and to some extent Enid's, reaction to Marjorie's conversation with Demos had diverted her attention. She had noticed Jo-Jo cornering Nellie Hurst soon after the performance, then Gladys Knott, and now he was with Myra. No doubt he had noticed the friction between her and Gladys and would be as keen as Rachel was to know how much they had veered off-script.

***

Waverley's office had been empty when Rachel went to see him, so she headed to the infirmary instead. Marjorie sat up in bed as soon as Rachel arrived, eyes alert and sparkling again.

"Tell me you have news on who tried to kill me?"

"Good to see you too," Rachel laughed. "How's she been, Bernard?"

Bernard giggled. "She became suddenly tired after I beat her twice at chess."

Marjorie wagged a finger at Bernard, whose wide grin forced his eyes to scrunch together, revealing prominent laughter lines. "Don't you be so cheeky, young man. It's not every day one is poisoned, as you well know."

Bernard held his hands up in mock defeat. "If you say so, Lady Marjorie. Can I leave you with the patient for five minutes?" he asked Rachel.

"Yes. Go ahead, I'll make sure she doesn't abscond while your back's turned."

Bernard left them to talk, his shoulders bobbing up and down from ongoing laughter. Rachel turned to Marjorie.

"I'm pleased to see you looking better."

"I'm absolutely fine, it's a waste of time and money keeping me in here overnight. I'm sure they've got better things to do."

Not wanting to get into an argument over Marjorie's stay, Rachel changed the subject. "I discovered a few interesting things this evening, but I'm not any closer to finding out who our poisoner is yet, unless Kate has joined forces with Demos. She's not at all happy you might take her Demos away via your…" Rachel formed air quotes with her index fingers, "…showbiz contacts."

Marjorie's lips tightened. "Silly girl, she's wasting her time with him."

"I agree, but she's more besotted than we imagined. Hardly spoke a word to me over dinner, and Enid was only mildly better. Then after the show, it all came out when I challenged Kate over her referring to you as my 'friend'."

"Well, I am your friend."

"Yes, but they – especially Kate – made a point of deliberately not mentioning your name. Anyway, there's a vicious side to that woman, and much of her repressed venom is headed in your direction at present. Plus, she stayed on board today while Enid went ashore."

Marjorie shook her head. "I can't envisage her wanting to kill me over that flighty gigolo."

"We can't rule it out. You didn't see her eyes – talk about green-eyed monster! I got the impression Enid might even suspect her daughter had something to do with the death of Dudley Bates."

"She can't have. She was nowhere near the stage on the night in question. Waverley won't have told them about the murder. He said he was going to inform Myra and the rest of the cast tomorrow, and he and Jason will interview them all again then."

"He hasn't; I told them. It just came out when Kate was going on about her precious Demos. It was obvious they already knew Dudley was dead and I let them know Demos had told you about the tragedy, then I implied he could have been murdered. That's when Enid reacted as though Kate might be involved."

"And if she was, which I still can't fathom, Demos has to be our killer. His Lordship's settled on the wife."

"Leanne? I'm not convinced because of what Jason said about their open marriage, but if she did do it, it could be about money rather than jealously. I don't know why, but I've got the feeling this murder and the attempt on your life are about jealously or love."

"Misplaced love, you mean?"

"Yes, which puts Kate and Demos right there in the frame."

"Did you get to speak to our silver-tongued gossip?"

"No. Before the show, the man I mentioned – the ex-cop, Jo-Jo Falconi – intercepted me. He definitely suspects foul play; I think it would be useful for him and me to put our heads together. He was busy after dinner, but I'll track him down tomorrow."

"You don't want my help, do you?" Marjorie's head dropped.

"It's not that, Marjorie. I almost lost you today; I was on my way to ask you if we could both take a backseat and leave it to the security team when I found you."

"Pah! Fat lot of use His Lordship would be. Jason, I grant you, uses his brain."

"You're too hard on the chief." Rachel took Marjorie's hand. "I'm serious, though. I really was hoping we could let it go, but I promise now I won't rest until I find who tried to poison you, no matter what Waverley says."

"Well, it's decided, then. We continue. I want to show whoever tried to kill me I'm very much alive and coming after them."

Rachel's mouth opened to argue, but the steely gaze in her friend's eyes told her she'd be wasting her time. She nodded.

"I think I'll stay on board tomorrow, while you're in here."

Marjorie raised her hand to argue. "No, Rachel. You were looking forward to going up the mountain with Sarah, and so was I. If you don't assure me you are going, I'll discharge myself."

Seeing her friend so adamant frightened Rachel. Whilst she was in the infirmary, Marjorie was safe.

"Okay, I'll go, but I won't enjoy myself on land without worrying about you. Anyway, I thought you didn't want to leave it all to Waverley."

"I don't," Marjorie conceded. "But you will go ashore, and you will enjoy yourself. Besides, I've been poisoned and I need some rest. I can't keep up with constant visitors."

Rachel's eyes widened before she burst out laughing. "Sometimes, Marjorie Snellthorpe, you're impossible."

"I'm entitled to be anything I like at my age," Marjorie countered.

Bernard returned and Rachel said goodnight to them both. She returned to her room, mulling over the evening's events in her mind.

"That's it!" she said out loud when a plan became clear. All she had to do was get Waverley to agree.

Chapter 20

Rachel had hardly slept, willing morning to come so she could set her plan in motion. She had almost paged Waverley in the middle of the night, but reasoned it would be counterproductive if she wanted to get him on side.

She dialled Sarah's room. The phone rang and rang before a tired answer came.

"Hello?"

"Sarah, it's me."

"Rachel. Is Marjorie okay?"

"Yes, yes, as far as I know. I left her in Bernard's capable hands last night."

"So why are you ringing me at six in the morning when we're not meeting 'til ten?"

"Sorry, but I need to speak to Waverley before he and Jason tell the Creations about the murder. Can you arrange it for 8am?"

Sarah groaned. "I suppose so, but why?"

"I'll explain at eight."

"So you want me to get up early on my day off and join you in some dubious plot to persuade Waverley to follow your – don't tell me – gut instinct about something?"

"That's about the sum of it. Will you?"

"Sure, as long as it doesn't get me the sack. Besides, it means I'll get to see Jason before we go ashore."

"You two lovebirds are sickening, you know that, don't you?"

"Yep, you'd better get used to it when we meet up after the wedding next year."

"Right, I'll warn Carlos."

"Who could be just as sickening a romantic if you'd let him," countered Sarah.

"Oh, trust me, I know, and I do let him when it suits."

"Rachel, you're unbearable. Now clear off if you want me to do your dirty work and be ready on time."

"Love you."

"Cupboard love," came the reply, but Rachel heard gaiety in her friend's voice as she put down the phone. The thing she loved most about Sarah was the fact she didn't brood for long, and because of her life as a cruise ship nurse, Sarah woke into thinking mode quicker than most.

Rachel leapt into action, running up the flight of stairs to deck sixteen to take in a few laps before returning to shower and dress in her casuals, ready for the day out. Her preference would have been to cancel the trip and not tell

Marjorie, but Sarah rarely got time off and, with Jason working, it wouldn't be fair on her.

She arrived outside Waverley's office on deck three five minutes early. The chief and Jason were already there, so she knocked.

"Come in, Rachel," Waverley called, sounding like he was in a good mood – for now, anyway. Sarah arrived on her heels as Rachel stepped inside. Waverley pointed to the armchairs around a coffee table, similar to those in Gwen's office. Jason gave her a grin before locking eyes with Sarah for a non-verbal moment of affection.

"What can I do for you, Rachel? Hopefully, you're here to tell me who tried to poison Lady Marjorie." Waverley laughed. He really was in a good mood.

"I was hoping you could tell me that," she replied.

"We'll be working on it today, along with telling Myra and the rest of the cast about the murder."

"About that—"

Waverley groaned audibly. "Rachel, I insist you and Lady Marjorie back off from the investigation now. Didn't she tell you?"

"I received your message from Marjorie, but hear me out, chief. I've come up with a plan and I think you'll like it."

"I doubt that very much. How about some coffee before you ruin my morning?"

Once they all had coffee in front of them, Rachel proceeded. "Last night I had dinner as usual with the two women who Marjorie and I have been sitting with. They both have a crush on one of the actors, Demos Benedict."

"The gossip, sir," interjected Jason.

"And a playboy from what I hear. What about it?"

Rachel explained how Marjorie had told Demos she had contacts within the film and theatre business, and how she might be able to help him. Then Rachel talked about Kate's reaction last night and how she might be dangerous.

"So you want us to interview them as well?" Waverley said. "Although I can't see how two passengers can be involved in this business, however gullible they might be."

Rachel wasn't so convinced about Kate's innocence, but let it pass. "That's not what I had in mind. Later in our conversation, I dropped the bombshell that I thought Dudley Bates might have been murdered to see if I got a reaction."

"And did you?" Waverley slurped his coffee. Rachel was pleased Marjorie wasn't here or he would have got a disapproving look.

"Yes, I did. I had already guessed Demos would have told them about the death, but wasn't sure whether or not he was involved, and I wanted to test Kate's reaction in case it implicated her. I got the impression Enid, Kate's mother, thought her daughter could be connected, but I can't be certain."

"So what are you asking me to do?" Waverley's patience was clearly running thin.

"They are the only ones who have been informed I suspect murder, and they're bound to tell Demos. If I'm right, he in turn will tell everyone else in the Creations world. My feeling is that when the killer finds out, they'll come after me before I can tell anyone else about my suspicions."

Three jaws dropped, and Sarah almost choked. "Are you saying what I think you're saying, Rachel Jacobi-Prince? That you want to put yourself out there as bait?"

Rachel was ready for the counterarguments and knew she would have to be persuasive. "If you tell the killer now you know about the murder, they'll be on their guard. Whoever is involved is wily and resourceful; they will cover their tracks big time."

Waverley stroked his chin. "Possibly, but we can be just as resourceful."

"I don't doubt it, but while they're thinking they've got away with murder, the killer's already been bold enough to have a go at Marjorie. If they realise you suspect poisoning, they won't carry out their masterplan."

"What masterplan?" scoffed Waverley.

"I don't know yet, but why attack Marjorie at all if they believe they've already got away with murder? Unless…" this was her trump card, the one that had come to her in the early hours, "…unless they plan to kill again."

Waverley shook his head, clearly finding it hard to comprehend what Rachel was getting at. "And what if they're not so clever as you think and they attacked Lady Marjorie to rid themselves of a nuisance nosy Parker?"

"In that case, they'll come after me as another loose end, won't they? Either way, we win; they'll drop their guard and make a mistake. When they do, we'll catch them."

"I can't risk it, Rachel. What if something were to happen to you?"

"Yes, Rachel, have you even considered the danger you'd be putting yourself in with a target on your back?" Sarah's voice shook and Rachel was regretting asking her to come along, but she needed her friend for the next part of her plan.

She put a hand on Sarah's shoulder. "I'll be careful. Besides, you'll be with me today, and Jason can keep an eye on me if we agree. Why don't we give it until the last show tomorrow night? I'm sure the killer will make a move by then."

"It makes sense, sir," said Jason, glancing apologetically towards Sarah as she grunted.

"I agree the strategy has some merit because – as you point out, Rachel – as soon as we start pushing, the killer may go dark. I'm willing to agree to this in principle as long as you accept we'll put a tail on you, and that you'll keep Lady Marjorie out of the loop."

"I expected you'd want to keep Marjorie safe, and so do I. That's where Sarah comes in. Can you persuade Dr

Bentley or your new friend Janet Plover to keep her in the infirmary until this is over?"

"I don't think it'll take much persuading. I'll speak to Graham, although he won't like your involvement in this dangerous plan." Sarah glared at Waverley and Jason. The latter dropped his eyes.

"Cool. Perhaps Jason could shadow me today?"

"Good idea," piped up Sarah, clearly forgetting her annoyance with her fiancé.

"I can agree to that, as we'll no longer be interviewing the Creations group today, and I'd rather someone I can trust kept an eye on you. Wear mufti, Goodridge."

"Yes, sir." Jason grinned.

"What if we see any of them on land?" Sarah queried.

"We won't. Myra Slade, or 'Blade' as the cast call her because of her sharp tongue, made it quite clear they are working for the duration and available at all times for guests to question them." Rachel was tempted again to bow out of the outing altogether and leave Sarah and Jason to themselves, but Waverley would cancel Jason's shore leave as fast as he'd granted it if she did.

Jason spoke. "There is just one thing, sir."

"Yes?"

"The woman I mentioned, Krystal Brewer. I was going to speak to her yesterday and ask her some questions because of her friendship with Benedict, but she was out all day. After Lady Marjorie was hospitalised, I thought I'd talk to her today and warn her to avoid all contact in case he's our man. Now, I don't know what to do."

"I can't put security on every guest, Goodridge," Waverley snapped.

"Sir, what if anything happens to her?"

Waverley sighed heavily. "Leave it with me. I'll give it some thought."

"Thank you, sir, It would mean a lot to me, especially after what happened to Lady Marjorie."

"Okay, Goodridge, you've made your point. Now go and get changed before I change my mind. Good day, ladies."

Taking that as their cue to vacate the room, Rachel and Sarah got up to leave. Rachel hoped she was doing the right thing, or this could be her last ever holiday.

***

During the ascent of over one thousand metres via the relatively new cable car to the summit of Mt Hoven, Rachel lost herself in the moment. It erased all thoughts of murder investigations from her mind as she took in the spectacular scenery. At the station on the mountain, there was a restaurant boasting 210-degree panoramic views. When they left the cable car at the top, the icy cold air caused their breath to fog. Sarah's SLR camera was out in an instant and she took the first track she could find.

"Wowser!" exclaimed Rachel as she followed her friend. "I don't think I've ever seen anything so beautiful."

Jason held onto the map they had been given at the bottom and pointed out important landmarks along the hike while Sarah, a keen amateur photographer, took photo after photo. They walked for forty minutes before Jason suggested they turn back and head to the restaurant for lunch.

"You can take in the rest of the views from the warm," he consoled Sarah.

Rachel was torn, but realised she really hadn't dressed for the cooler temperatures up the mountain, having been too busy setting in place her masterplan.

"It would be warmer inside," she agreed, shivering.

"The trouble with you is you never listen," scolded Sarah. "Too busy exercising your little grey cells, as Poirot would say. I told you to wear a padded windbreaker, but no, you put on a light fleece."

"Tell you what, I'll jog back to warm up. You two can share some quality time."

"Is that wise?" asked Jason. "I'm supposed to keep a watch over you."

"I don't think there's any killer up here – apart from the cold, if I stay still for much longer. See you back at the restaurant. Take your time; I'll ring Carlos when I get there and send him some photos."

Rachel took off before either of them could argue. She was pleased to be moving and would make it back much quicker if she didn't have to keep stopping for every photo opportunity. Once Sarah got going, there was no holding her back, and this was her first visit up here, too.

The Queen of Norway had officially opened the Loen Cable Car in 2017, the guide had told them on the way up. Marjorie had been looking forward to the spectacle, but hid her disappointment well when Dr Bentley told her she must stay in the infirmary for another day. Rachel suspected she'd believed he would discharge her this morning, which he might have done had he not had a conversation with Sarah.

Rachel arrived back at the front of the restaurant within fifteen minutes, but halted when she saw a couple alone on a precipice not too far away. The man was down on one knee. Rachel smiled at the reminder of the moment Carlos had proposed. The woman obviously said yes, as the man placed a ring on her finger and they turned towards the trail Rachel had just returned from.

Well, well, Myra got her wish after all, Rachel thought, recognising the couple walking arm in arm, chatting excitedly. Rachel wondered how the domineering Gladys Knott had taken the news, or had Cody kept it a secret?

As another crowd gathered in front of the restaurant after arriving by cable car, Rachel walked inside and ordered a hot mocha before finding a table with a spectacular view over Jostedalsbreen Glacier. She pressed speed dial and the familiar voice answered.

"You must have read my mind. I was about to call you," Carlos said cheerily.

"How are things in bonnie Scotland?" she asked.

"Cold in every way."

"Does that mean you've not found the girl?"

"Not yet. I'm working on a lead from one of her friends. Seems she got chatting to someone online and arranged to meet him. She swore her friend to secrecy, saying her parents would go ape. I've involved an old friend who's digging into her digital signature and checking the guy is who he said he was; I'll know more this evening. Her friend did tell me where she thought the couple were heading. Lady and I will be there in a couple of hours, but I'm told phone signals are bad up there. How's things with you?"

"Also cold. I'm up a mountain. I wish you could see these views, Carlos. We have to come back here together."

"Now you're talking. Is Marjorie with you?"

"No, she's tired. It would be too cold up here for her, anyway. Sarah and Jason are here, but Sarah's snapping pictures all the time so I'm sitting in a nice warm restaurant, drinking a nice hot mocha, looking over a glacier and missing my husband."

"And I you. I'll be having a hot toddy when we stop. Signal's not great now, I'm on speakerphone, but I miss you too. I'll call you tonight if either of us has a signal."

"Okay, darling. I love you."

"I love you too, Rachel. Give Marjorie and Sarah a hug from me."

"What about Jason?"

"Give him a bro hug! Ciao." He laughed as he disconnected. Rachel smiled at the phone.

"I bet you didn't tell him what you're up to." Sarah's voice dragged her from her reverie.

"No time. He's driving."

"Yep. If you say so."

"How about some lunch?" Jason offered, clearly wanting to keep Sarah as happy as possible. Both women nodded.

"You'll never guess who we just passed?"

"Myra and Cody?" Rachel smirked.

"You can be really annoying at times, Rachel, you know that? They seemed thrilled. Jason pulled his hat over his face – not that they noticed him, totally wrapped up in each other."

"They've just got engaged."

"And you know that because?"

"Because I saw it happen, but they didn't see me, so all's good."

"I'm surprised you didn't leap out and say, 'Here I am, kill me'," Sarah bantered.

"I think Nurse Bradshaw needs to eat, Jason, before she gets any grouchier."

Jason leaned down and kissed Sarah on the forehead. "Everything will work out, I promise."

Rachel hoped he was right.

Chapter 21

After they got back to the ship, Rachel went to visit Marjorie and Sarah had to change for work, so Jason returned to his room to shower and change. Once he was back in uniform, he headed down to the main security office to check the work board. Thankfully, no new crimes had been committed while he was off the ship.

The *Coral Queen* had state-of-the-art computers and surveillance equipment available if required, but always as a last resort and only if evidence supported its use. Passenger privacy remained the cruise line's mantra and head office would fire anyone who abused any equipment on board. All security officers carried tasers, with guns and other heavy-duty defence weapons kept locked away at all times. Every day, a member of security checked the weapons locker to see that nothing was missing and everything was in working order. The checks were logged in the equipment book. Sarah had told Jason they had similar procedures within the medical team regarding medicines and equipment.

Jason glanced at the log, a habit he had not been able to shake since leaving the army. It did no harm to double-check. Satisfied all was good, he poured himself a coffee from a flask and sat at the station before pressing a few keys on the keyboard. Bringing a computer to life, he entered his username and password.

He scanned through the background checks of all the members of the Murder Mystery Creations again, paying particular attention to Demos Benedict and Leanne Bates. There was nothing pointing to either of them being a cold-hearted killer, but that didn't prove innocence. It could mean they had never been either caught or pushed far enough to kill before. Demos had admitted to Jason he'd dabbled with drugs at acting college, but, Jason reasoned, Deadly Nightshade was not on a junkie's wish list, so it seemed unlikely he would know much about it. Leanne had never been caught using drugs, whereas her husband had.

He tapped on a few keys to request access to the cast members' education background and CVs. It was time to dig deeper. He pulled up Nellie Hurst's record; she'd remained under the radar with no suspicion pointing towards her. There was nothing to be found. Her record was clean.

This case needed legwork and it was frustrating not being able to interview the suspects more thoroughly, even though Rachel's argument for discretion made sense. Jason wanted to push their buttons and see what came out. He had to admit, Rachel and Lady Marjorie had discovered quite a bit in terms of who might have a motive, and the boss was pretty certain the wife had done it. Jason was keeping an open mind, but leaned towards Demos Benedict. The only two who would know about atropine for certain were the doctor and the vet, but neither of them had any reason to kill Dudley Bates; they'd only recently met when Cody started dating Myra Slade.

Rachel said she'd witnessed a proposal between the Creations' lovebirds at the top of the mountain. Jason smiled as he remembered his own stumbling effort last Christmas, when he'd asked Sarah to marry him after months of deliberation. She was the best thing that had happened to him, and he couldn't wait for the spring when they would get married. He just hoped he didn't blow it.

Shaking the thought from his head, he turned towards a noise as the door opened.

"Enjoy your time ashore?" Waverley asked, pouring himself a coffee.

"It was spectacular up there – what views!" Jason answered.

"Thought you'd like it; Brenda and I went up last year. Cold at this time of year, I expect?"

"Not if you're dressed properly, which Rachel wasn't," Jason laughed. "Sarah's penchant for stopping to take photos every two seconds made the cold even worse for her."

Waverley chuckled. "At least she's safe, for now. Where is she?"

"In the infirmary visiting Lady Marjorie. I wondered about giving her an earpiece and radio mic so we can keep tabs on her, if it's allowed?"

"I had the same idea. Yes, give her one; at least that way you'll know where she is and what she's up to. She can turn it off when she's in her room. I'm thinking of putting a man outside her door."

"She won't like that."

"Then she shouldn't make herself a target, should she?" Waverley snapped. Jason was thinking it would remove the element of surprise Rachel was after, but thought he'd leave her to argue that one with Waverley.

"We saw Myra and Cody Spark up on the mountain today."

"I thought they were working?"

"I suppose when you're the boss, you can do as you like. No offence, sir. We passed them on our way back up to the restaurant. Rachel had gone ahead to warm up and witnessed a proposal."

Waverley grinned. He'd been much more pro-marriage since his wedding with Brenda, prior to which he'd been a cynic after his wife left him for another man, a friend of his. Best friends could become worst enemies when it came to women – or men, for that matter.

"So he's gone against Mummy, then."

"In fairness, Dr Knott is probably not that bad, just overprotective. Let's hope so, anyway, otherwise Myra's in for a rough ride with the mother-in-law."

Waverley laughed. "I think Myra Slade – or is it Blade? – is quite capable of managing an evil mother-in-law. What about you, Goodridge?"

"Sarah's mum's a piece of cake; it's mine who'll be the problem." Jason had a troubled relationship with his parents, who had a history of drinking too much and were currently in rehab. He hadn't even wanted to invite them to the wedding, but Sarah had insisted, and to their credit, his mum and dad were hoping to make it.

"It'll all work out for you and Sarah, and if your parents… erm, backslide, you've still got each other and her family."

Jason wasn't comfortable talking about a personal matter with his boss, so he moved on. "Anything to report here, sir? How's Krystal?"

"Sorry, Goodridge, we haven't been able to follow her. She'd already left ship when I had a man spare, but I've just checked and she's back on board. I don't think you need to worry about her; seems like she's taken your advice and is enjoying her cruise."

"I still don't like her association with Benedict, sir, not until we can be certain he's not our man. I'll have a word with her steward to let me know when she's in her room, then pop in for a cup of tea."

"Do what you think necessary, but I can't spare anyone else for surveillance at the minute. Speaking of which, did you know the cameras were out on the corridor where the Creations are staying?"

Jason frowned. "That can't be a coincidence."

"I spoke to maintenance, who said they've been out for a couple of weeks. Apparently the entire system's been playing up intermittently because of a fault in that corridor. They isolated it and switched off until they could understand it. They have repaired it today."

"Why didn't we know about it?"

Waverley coughed and his face flushed crimson. "Erm, I yelled at the head of maintenance, demanding to know the same thing. He showed me a copy of a report sent a couple of weeks back. I, erm, found it in my in-tray."

Jason couldn't help despairing at his boss sometimes. The man was old school and hated paperwork. Normally, it wouldn't be an issue and probably wasn't now. CCTV in passenger corridors had been a reluctant addition to the ship's security following an increase in opportunistic crime and murder on board the *Coral*. Running security on a ship was like managing a small town, but with a constant change in population, and was no simple task. Repairing CCTV cameras wouldn't be top of the maintenance team's priority list, either, as the smooth running of the ship and passenger comfort always came first.

"It wouldn't tell us anything, anyway, especially as Krystal is safe. One of the stateroom stewards saw her going into Benedict's room the other night."

"I don't think you have anything to worry about there. Even if he is our killer, she's his friend."

Jason rubbed his temples, unable to shake off his concern about the woman he felt responsible for.

"Nevertheless, I'll have a word."

"Do what you've got to do. I'm going for dinner, are you coming?"

"I had a big lunch, so no. I'll catch up with Krystal, and then Rachel before the penultimate act in the Cocktail Lounge. I might just hang about around there tonight, if that's okay?"

"I was going to put Ravanos in there, but if you want to do it, you've got it."

"Thank you, sir. I'll take it."

***

Maria, the room steward for deck eight, port side aft, was pushing her evening trolley along the corridor when Jason called out to her.

"Good evening, Maria, can you let me know when Mrs Brewer's back from dinner? I'd like another word with her."

"I'll try, sir, but I haven't seen her for two days."

"What do you mean, two days?" Jason felt his heart rate rising.

Maria held out her hands, palms up. "She's had a 'do not disturb' sign up since yesterday morning. I've knocked twice today, but there's been no reply. I've been looking out for her and asked my assistant to try to catch her, too; I don't like leaving passenger rooms unattended for this long. I was hoping the sign would be down tonight, but it's still there."

"Thanks, Maria. I'll leave you to get on."

Jason felt a tightness in his chest as he marched along the lengthy corridor towards room 8337. He knocked twice, but when there was no reply, he used his universal pass to open the door, dreading the worst.

The room was in darkness with drapes pulled across the balcony. "Mrs Brewer… Krystal? It's Jason Goodridge, security." No reply. He flicked on the lights with his card and walked along the short corridor to the main bed-sitting room. He held his breath as he checked both sides of the bed, followed by the balcony. Nothing. The bed was made up for night-time and hadn't been slept in.

Glancing around the room, he noted a nightdress placed neatly on top of the pillow, with leaflets and the *Coral News* laid on the bed. He picked up the daily which was given to all passengers each night, packed with the next day's activities. His pulse quickened again when he noted this one was yesterday's, meaning she hadn't returned to her room since David, the deck nine steward, had seen her with Demos Benedict.

Stepping outside, Jason checked the plastic rack where advertising leaflets for special events and offers were placed for passengers. Behind an A4 leaflet for a mega sale of Swarovski crystal, he found today's *Coral News*, which would have been placed there last night. He went back into the room and opened wardrobes and drawers. As he'd expected, Krystal's clothes were still there. He checked the bathroom, noting a toiletry bag was open on the shelf. Then he left the room and walked gloomily down the corridor.

"Is everything okay, sir?" Maria called.

"Not sure yet, Maria. Don't go into the room until Mrs Brewer returns or I say it's all right."

Maria's eyes widened. She was clearly concerned, but there was nothing he could say at present.

"Is Mrs Brewer in trouble, sir?"

"Not at all. Don't worry, Maria, she might be a night owl. She's been off ship today and yesterday, so I'm sure we'll track her down. Let me know immediately if you see her, though."

Jason called reception on his radio. As he took the stairs down to the atrium, he heard the ship-wide announcement.

"Please, could Mrs Krystal Brewer come to main reception? Please could Mrs Brewer come to main reception? Thank you."

Jason stood at reception for half an hour while repeated calls went out. With every unanswered call, his heart sank; he dreaded what could have happened to his mischievous charge and blamed himself for her disappearance. As guilt weighed heavily, it threatened to cloud his judgement.

Chapter 22

Marjorie's patience with having to remain in the infirmary was wearing thin, so Rachel stayed for longer than she'd intended, trying to distract her through humour. However, her friend remained disgruntled.

"I'd much prefer to be with you tonight rather than leaving you to face hostility from Kate on your own. I've thought about it throughout the day. What if she is dangerous?"

"I've considered it, too, Marjorie, and I don't believe she is. She's jealous, yes, but even if Demos is incriminated, I can't see him getting her to do anything dodgy. It would be too risky. Besides, she's devoted to her mother, and underneath it all, she's just blinded by her obsession."

"Exactly. And obsession can lead to dangerous outcomes."

Rachel hesitated. "I'll be careful, I promise. Waverley has someone covering my back, so I'll be fine."

Marjorie relented. "Interesting about Myra and the vet, isn't it? I didn't think he'd have it in him to go against his mother."

"Perhaps she's approved the match, realising that a parent should beware before trying to stand between a couple in love, or she might end up losing him altogether."

"Yes, I suspect she's conceded ungraciously," Marjorie laughed. "I can't see the formidable Dr Knott doing otherwise."

Rachel agreed. From what she'd seen and heard about the manipulative doctor and after the performance on stage last night, she guessed the woman wouldn't have given in without a fight.

"I bet that's what the tension on stage last night was all about. Cody must have told his mother before the performance. No wonder she went off piste with her lines – she and Myra were at each other like a pair of street cats."

"Oh, I do wish I'd been there to see it, and to protect you from Kate's vicious streak. I'm surprised Enid was off with you, though."

"Only a little; I think her attraction to Demos is of a more realistic kind than her daughter's. Nevertheless, there's no way I'll risk asking her to press Demos for information now, just in case her loyalty swings more his way."

"I agree with you there, best not. Perhaps Jo-Jo's the one to work with. I don't know why His Lordship's changed his mind and is no longer investigating himself; he was so adamant last night."

"I guess he slept on it." Rachel hated deceiving Marjorie, but if the older lady knew what she was up to, she'd insist on putting herself in danger.

"When I see young Dr Bentley later, I'm going to insist on being discharged. I'm as fit as he is." Marjorie's eyes flashed and Rachel thought it better to tackle this argument later. She checked her watch. It was almost time to change if she was going to have any time before dinner to quiz the cast and speak with Jo-Jo.

"I'd better be going. Good idea about Jo-Jo, I'll have a chat with him."

Marjorie relaxed back onto her pillows. "At least that's something."

Rachel had no intention of involving Jo-Jo for the same reason she wanted Marjorie safely ensconced in the infirmary, but she would like to pick his brains about what he knew. As she stood to leave, an announcement rang out.

"Please, could Mrs Krystal Brewer come to main reception? Please could Mrs Brewer come to main reception? Thank you."

"Isn't that the woman Jason mentioned the other night?" quizzed Marjorie. "I hope nothing's happened to her now."

Rachel's heart sank and she hoped the same thing. "It could be anything." She tried to sound more reassuring than she felt. "I'll call in after the show this evening and give you the lowdown."

"Goodie. At least I have that to look forward to. Any idea who's looking after this old biddy this evening?"

"Gwen said she'll be popping in and out now you're a bit better. The others will be in surgery; I think Bernard's on call, so no chess this evening. See you later."

"Bye, dear." Marjorie's voice sounded glum, but despite feeling guilty, Rachel held her resolve. She debated whether to go to reception to see what the callout was for, but decided she didn't have time. She just hoped nothing had happened to Krystal Brewer while Jason had been ashore. It would be a hard knock for him.

Sarah had told her why Jason took his responsibility so seriously: he suffered from survivor guilt from his time in Afghanistan. One day, he had been due to go on a patrol with his team when he dislocated his shoulder playing rugby in the barracks. A replacement joined the patrol and their vehicle was blown up by a roadside bomb. His four friends died instantly, along with his replacement. It had been a hard blow and had given Jason nightmares ever since. If something had happened to Krystal, Rachel was all too aware how that would bring Jason's horrific memories back to the surface.

Being married to an ex-soldier who carried his own baggage had taught Rachel just how difficult it was for the armed forces' men and women to readjust to civilian life. Even when things were going well, little triggers could invade their subconscious. Others wouldn't recognise these triggers, so no-one else would know what was going on. She sent up a quick prayer for Krystal and Jason before rushing back to her room.

***

Lively music greeted Rachel as she made her way into the Cocktail Lounge, which was packed as usual with eager sleuths keen to win the prizes on offer, and to be proven right. She heard some discussions as she made her way towards Demos, determined not to be cut off this evening as people argued over who might have done it. Most seemed convinced it was Toni Cleeves, the lounge singer, played by Nellie Hurst, or Dora Michaels the duchess's sister, played by Leanne Bates. Rachel hadn't given the fictional murder much thought, but wondered why no-one suspected the duchess herself or the grandson Sly Toner, played by Demos Benedict.

Rachel sideswiped her way to face Demos, who didn't seem as popular this evening. Once she got next to him, she could tell why. He reeked of alcohol and was obviously drinking more than usual.

"Hi," Rachel held out her hand. "I'm Rachel, can I have a word?"

His glazed eyes looked her up and down and paused for longer than she felt comfortable with over her breasts. She prodded his chin up with her finger, forcing him to look at her face.

"Sure, anytime." His bleary eyes seemed unhappy.

"Why don't we find a seat somewhere?" Rachel said, taking his arm and directing the unsteady man over to the bar. "Coffee, please," she said to the barman.

Demos raised a hand to protest, but didn't.

"Make it black," said Rachel, "and two bottles of water."

The barman nodded, understanding.

"You're quite forceful, aren't you? What did you say your name was?" Demos slurred.

"Rachel. I've heard all about you from Enid and Kate, and I think you spoke to my friend, Lady Snellthorpe."

"Yesh," he raised his head. "She's going to help me. Kate's not keen – fancies me, you know. I prefer her mother – she's hot."

"I bet you get that a lot," said Rachel.

Demos tried to straighten up. Rachel offered him a bottle of water, which he took and thankfully downed in one.

"I do, 'scept the one I want's gone and got engaged."

Rachel's eyebrows rose. "Really? Who's that?" she asked, already guessing the answer.

"Her over there." Rachel followed his eyes to where Myra was dishing out instructions to crew members setting up the stage. "We were good together, we was."

"You went out with Myra Slade?" Rachel placed a mug of black coffee in his hands and he drank.

"More than that. We were gonna get married 'til Dudley blinking Bates got off with her."

"Is Dudley the man who died?"

"Yeah, and good riddance to 'im." Demos held up his empty coffee mug in a toast. "To the dead that got their just reward." Rachel handed him a full mug of coffee the barman had brought over to her.

"You were glad to see him dead, then?" She fixed her gaze on his bleary, bloodshot eyes.

"Too right I was. He cost me everything: my woman and my promotion."

Rachel wondered which of the two was the more important to him. "Yes, Enid told me about your promised promotion. She feels sorry for you."

"She's nice, a good listener. So's your friend Lady shnell..."

"Snellthorpe," Rachel offered. She lowered her voice. "I understand Dudley's death was suspicious, that he might have been murdered."

"So Kate told me today, says some busybody called Rachel told her. Hang on, did you say your name was Rachel?"

"Yes, Rachel Busybody, pleased to meet you." She flashed a disarming smile and handed him another bottle of water. The coffee and water were having the desired effect.

He grinned. "I expected an ugly duckling, not a beautiful swan," he took her hand. "Ooh, married, I see. Not that it matters these days."

"It matters to me." She pulled her hand away. "I thought you'd just had your heart broken?"

"I didn't say that."

"You're right, you used the word want rather than love. I should have known."

"Known what?"

"Never mind. Back to the topic of Dudley Bates: do you think it possible he was murdered?"

"Not sure. I've been asking around among the cast. None of them think he was, but you never know: a bloke like him had a lot of enemies."

"Such as?"

"Myra for one. Once he put his money in the business, he wanted more of a say than she was willing to give him. She was furious the day we boarded 'cos he told her if she didn't comply, he'd pull the money out again…"

"Could he have done that?"

"Seems so. He added a clause to the contract she didn't pick up on – not so clever after all, our Myra blooming Slade soon to be Spark." He chuckled.

"Who else didn't like him?"

"His wife, Leanne, despised him for being into drugs and for all his playing around."

"Was she jealous?"

"No. Me and Leanne are two of a kind; it's more pride with us. Then there's Nellie."

Rachel's ears pricked up. That name hadn't been on her radar at all.

"Nellie Hurst?"

"Yeah. She had the hots for our Dudley. They had a one-night stand, but she couldn't let it go, told everyone they were going out. He was livid with her, told her if she kept shooting her mouth off, he'd get her fired. As if he stood a chance, her being Myra's cousin and all."

"And what about Cody?"

"That wimp? Not sure he even knows how much Myra put it about to get her own way. I'll soon put him right there. I'm amazed he had the guts to propose to her, though. Let's have another toast." Demos looked hopefully towards the barman, who held out a third mug of coffee. "Point taken." Demos took the mug and lifted it in the air. "To wimps who grow balls."

"What about you? You said he took your woman – did you hate Dudley Bates enough to kill him?"

Demos stared at her, wide-eyed. "Me? No, I don't do violence, except on stage. I prefer wooing the ladies; speaking of which—"

"No chance," she said, pushing his hand away. "It's been a pleasure talking to you. I expect some of your fan club would like a word now you're sober."

Demos turned to see a group of women standing in line behind him. He winked at Rachel before turning away again.

"Good evening, ladies. How gorgeous you all look tonight."

Nauseating, thought Rachel, leaving him to his crowd of admirers.

Chapter 23

Rachel spotted a gloomy-looking Jason standing at the edge of the room. She wished she could speak to him and ask about Krystal Brewer, but didn't want people – especially the cast – to see they were acquainted.

Jo-Jo was talking to Leanne Bates, so she waited for him to finish, and for Leanne's attention to turn elsewhere, before tapping him on the arm.

"Good evening, Jo-Jo. How are you getting on?"

"Very well, as a matter of fact. I've just about deduced whodunnit – well, narrowed it down to two, anyways."

Rachel dropped her voice, "I was wondering if I could take a look at the footage from your mobile phone? Celia May told me you recorded some of the first night's act, the one that's missing."

"Sure you can, but it won't help you much. I've gone over it a dozen times. Here." He unlocked his phone and handed it to her. "I just want a word with Nellie Hurst before dinner. I'll trust you to hand it back, Officer." He winked. Rachel grinned back and took herself off to the restroom to view the footage. Pleased they had the same phone type, she plugged in her earphones.

The video was, as Jo-Jo had said, not particularly useful. During the part when the drinks were handed out and Dudley, aka Marvin Black, went to the bar to get one after finding the tray empty, the footage was focussed on Demos, aka Sly Toner. At least she could rule him out for certain, as he was the first to grab a glass from the tray and didn't move out of shot. The rest of the cast, alas, did.

People were making their way to tables by the time she returned to the Cocktail Lounge, so she sidled over to where Jo-Jo and Celia May were sitting and handed over the phone.

"I thank you, mam," he said. "Anything useful?"

"Not really, but thanks for the loan."

"We need to put our heads together, if you're thinking what I'm thinking," Jo-Jo replied.

Celia May frowned. "Jo-Jo, I've warned you about this. Now just stop."

He mouthed, "Later," to Rachel.

Rachel found Enid and Kate in a much happier frame of mind than they'd been the previous evening, so dinner turned out to be a better experience than she'd expected. At least until they'd finished eating.

"Have you found your killer yet?" Kate mocked.

"Don't joke about such things, Kate," Enid chastised her daughter. "I don't know what's got into you this week."

I do, thought Rachel, but she said, "Still working on it. You?"

The women stared, open-mouthed.

"Oh, you mean the death of Dudley Bates," said Rachel. "I thought you meant Marvin Black. It's too much for my brain to take in."

"Don't play the innocent with us. I saw you talking to that ex-cop over there, and to Demos earlier. We told him what you said."

Rachel was concerned they knew Jo-Jo was an ex-police officer; that was sure to have got back to the killer. She kicked herself for being so obvious about talking to him.

"Told who what I said about what?"

"Demos, of course. I told him about you saying someone could have murdered Dudley Bates."

"And what did he have to say about it?"

"You tell us. You were having a nice, long private chinwag at the bar earlier, weren't you?" Nasty Kate appeared to have come out of her box again.

"I was helping him sober up, or he'd never have got up on stage tonight. He was upset about Myra's engagement to Cody Spark."

That comment hit the mark. Kate screwed her face up accusingly. "Why should he be upset about such a thing? If they are engaged at all, that is. You seem to be getting a lot of inside information all of a sudden."

Rachel was tiring of the Jekyll and Hyde nature of Kate and spoke directly to Enid. "You mentioned Myra had a fling with Dudley; apparently, she also had one with Demos." Turning back to Kate, she said, "Not to worry, I don't believe he was emotionally invested. It was just his pride that was hurt." She resisted saying how much he liked Enid, not wanting to cause friction between the two women.

"I see," said Enid.

"I didn't know the elderly gentleman had been in the police force. I got talking to his wife the other evening, and she recommended one of the hairdressers on board. I couldn't remember the name, that's all."

"Whatever you say," snapped Kate. "I need the loo before the show starts. Mum, are you coming?"

Enid glanced apologetically towards Rachel, and Rachel heard her admonishing her daughter for her behaviour. As they walked away, Rachel stared into her glass as her concern for Jo-Jo grew.

How could I have been so stupid?

***

Myra struck Rachel as understandably euphoric this evening, even laughing and joking with the cast before the penultimate act started. The problem was that none of the others, apart from Cody and, surprisingly, Gladys Knott, were sharing her joy. In fact, they were more long-faced than usual. Perhaps they didn't relish change.

It was odd watching the group from the outside, like a play within a play. The only conclusion Rachel could come to was that they were a mismatched, dysfunctional lot.

With her usual sunny disposition, Tatum introduced Act Four, cracking jokes and reminding passengers of the multitudinous delights the *Coral Queen* had on offer. Had she been there, Marjorie would have commented that the cruise line worked hard to squeeze every last penny out of its passengers while they were on board.

Act Four comprised more of the same arguing and finger-pointing. The chief of security blundered around, trying to get to the bottom of the crime and frequently jumping to the wrong conclusions. Rachel chuckled to herself, imagining the comparisons Marjorie would make between the fictional chief and the real one.

The ship's doctor, played again by Myra, seemed to be getting closer to unravelling the plot. It was obvious as the tension mounted that she herself would soon be in danger. Gladys seemed happy throughout the performance and appeared to stick to her lines, which drew shared smiles between Myra and Cody, hardly noticeable to anyone who didn't know they were an item. Perhaps the old woman was pleased for her son after all, and the others had misinterpreted her protective nature as domineering.

But why is she so protective? Rachel made a note to ask Jason about Cody's past, realising she knew little about him other than he worked as a vet and had never married. Maybe someone had broken his heart in the past, causing Gladys to overreact.

What one of us hasn't met with heartbreak? she mused.

The scene ended as the doctor slammed her laptop shut and spoke out loud.

"Gotcha! Now all I have to do is prove it," she announced as the curtain closed.

Rapturous cheers and hand clapping followed the performance as per usual, along with whistles and shouting for more. Demos had sobered up enough to play the part of the petulant grandson well, and Kate and Enid never took their eyes off him throughout the performance as far as Rachel could tell.

After the final bow, the cast remained on stage while Myra held a microphone to her mouth.

"Well, ladies and gentlemen, I hope you are enjoying your sleuthing. Many of you have approached me with names of people you think did the deed." A ripple of laughter spread through the room. "I can neither confirm nor deny your suspicions, as I've said from the beginning, but I will say that some of you are right," she teased to further laughter, followed by a short round of applause.

"As you know, tomorrow will be the last act of 'Murder on Deck'. When you return to your staterooms, you will find cards in your post, which you will need to complete and post in a special box that has been placed in reception. Please do this by tomorrow noon. We will set aside the cards with correct answers, and when we reveal the killer during tomorrow night's show, you'll know if you got it right.

"Following the show, Tatum Rodman, your assistant cruise director, will manage the draw and the winner will be announced and invited to the stage. As a bonus, the winner will join the cast backstage for drinks and a light meal. Thank you and goodnight."

Further applause followed, and within minutes, the cast was mingling with the crowd. Enid and Kate put their heads together and were discussing who they believed the killer was when Demos joined their table. Both women flashed him enormous smiles, but it was Rachel's hand he took.

"Thank you for your help earlier. I apologise if my behaviour was in any way inappropriate."

Rachel withdrew her hand. "It was nothing; the performance was great."

"I was hoping to have a word with your friend, Lady Marjorie. Is she here?"

Ah, I should have known the apology was an act. Any empathy she had felt for the man soon dissipated.

"She's not, I'm afraid, but I'll share your request when I see her." *Not,* she added silently. Rachel smiled at Kate, whose glaring eyes were shooting daggers in her direction. "Goodnight, I look forward to our finale tomorrow."

Rachel headed out of the Cocktail Lounge, passing Jason on her way. He bent down to pick something up.

"Madam?"

She turned, "Yes?"

"I think you dropped this."

Rachel took a small black wallet, registering the subterfuge. "So I did. Thank you."

She examined the contents as she walked down the stairs to the infirmary: a radio transmitter and earpiece. She closed the wallet, deep in thought. Something out of sync had happened tonight and she needed to investigate. This could be the key to the murder.

Chapter 24

Jo-Jo Falconi was convinced there was something to investigate about the so-called natural death of the actor from the night they boarded. He'd found out about the death from the talkative Demos Benedict, who couldn't keep a secret if his life depended on it, but every time he tried to quiz the other thespians, they clammed up, saying they didn't know what he was talking about. Demos in particular was snarky about the dead man, but then he didn't seem to like any of the others, either. The ex-wife was defensive.

Now, going through the video from the opening night for the umpteenth time, Jo-Jo was convinced he knew who the murderer was. He could kick himself for not moving the recording away from the Benedict fella just before the murder, meaning he had no proof. Celia May was doing better than he was with interviewing the cast and they were gradually pulling together a picture of what had happened. The only concern he had was that he could be mistaking a plain and simple death by natural causes for a felony.

"Celia May, can we go over these suspects again?"

"I hope you mean the ones for 'Murder on Deck', Jo-Jo, because I'm worried you're going to do serious damage to your blood pressure if you don't learn to distinguish fiction from fact. You know what the doctor told you before we came on this cruise: rest and relaxation, he ordered. I thought this event would help exercise your mind without you seeing murderers under every tree."

"You're not being fair," Jo-Jo huffed. "I'm telling you something's not right here. One of those people is a murderer and I think I know who it is."

"Jo-Jo, the ship's doctor says the man died of natural causes. Even that loudmouth, Demos Benedict, says the same. Why can't you just accept it?"

"Celia May, my nose is telling me there's foul play here. Now are you going to help me or not?" he snapped. He'd been a lot more irritable recently. The pain in his knee kept him awake most nights, but he refused sleeping pills. Just before the cruise, his doctor had told him his blood pressure was too high and the indigestion he'd been getting was angina. He hated getting old; he felt so useless.

"I'm not," Celia May snapped back, which was unlike her. She was clearly feeling the strain of his ill health. "Jo-Jo, I love you, have done for fifty years, but if you don't drop this, I'm flying home tomorrow."

Jo-Jo's mouth opened to counter, but he thought better of it. Instead, he got up and headed for the stateroom door.

"I'm going for a walk."

"At this time of night? Now you're being ridiculous."

He glared back at his wife before storming out. If the damn door wasn't on some sort of spring, he would have slammed it.

He limped along the corridor towards the elevator, already regretting his outburst. Celia May was right: he should drop it. Even if there was something odd going on, he was too old and too unfit for this game. When the elevator arrived, he considered turning back, but pride dictated he should at least stay away for a little while, if only to calm down.

A young couple in the elevator were gazing adoringly into each other's eyes, desire oozing from them as they smooched. He remembered that feeling well enough. What he and Celia May had now was so much better than the early passion, although they still enjoyed each other; they were soulmates and he loved her more now than ever. He didn't know what he'd do without her.

By the time he got out of the elevator on the Lido Deck and pulled the door open to get some fresh air, he was resolved to follow his wife's advice. He would pass on what he knew to that nice young woman, Rachel, who he was sure was of the same opinion as he was. She would know what to do.

He shivered as he walked along the outside deck, taking in the fresh but freezing night air. Clouds hid the stars, usually beautiful at night in this part of the world. He paused for a moment before deciding to turn back. Would

Celia May really fly home without him? He needed to get back and apologise.

Hurrying as fast as his knee would allow without his stick, he heard a sound behind him. He turned on his good leg.

"You!" he uttered as he felt the kick to his bad leg that sent him reeling down a small set of steps. "Celia May, I'm so sorry," he whispered as the last thoughts entering his head before everything went black were of his gorgeous wife.

***

Marjorie was being her usual stubborn self, insisting on being discharged from the infirmary.

"I'm not staying here for a third night. I've missed two shows and I'm not missing the finale. We still need to find this killer."

"*We* will do no such thing, Marjorie," snapped Rachel. "I'm not letting you out of my sight. It's too dangerous. Whoever it is has already tried to kill you once."

"I'm not frightened of dying, Rachel. But I am frightened of not living. You of all people should understand that."

Rachel's eyes met Sarah's, appealing for help.

"She's right, you know," Sarah said.

"See?" said Rachel triumphantly.

"No, I mean Marjorie's right. Normally I would be with you on this, but Marjorie hates being cooped up."

"Seriously? Has everyone taken leave of their senses?"

Marjorie patted Sarah's hand and gazed smugly towards Rachel.

"I don't mean you should involve yourself in a murder investigation, Marjorie, but Graham agrees you're fit enough to be discharged. Anyway, Waverley's taking over." Sarah locked onto Rachel's eyes, the unspoken words saying that as long as Marjorie thought Waverley was in charge, they wouldn't have to worry about her.

"Good," said Rachel. "Let him get on with it. Okay, Marjorie, you win. I'll go and get you some fresh clothes. I'll come back for you in half an hour."

"I'm a little peckish, dear. Erm… I was in a tizz when Raggie brought dinner and I told him to take it away."

"Having a tantrum, more like," Rachel rolled her eyes, but grinned despite herself. "I'll stop by the buffet on the way back, as long as you don't complain about buffet food."

Marjorie's eyes sparkled. "I could eat a horse."

Sighing, Rachel headed out.

Sarah followed her to the door. "Sorry."

"Don't be. You're right and I'd be just the same if I was her. At least this way I'll know exactly where she is."

"And are you going to continue with the mad plan you agreed?"

"Yes, of course. I'm still alive thus far. Anyway, I think I've got an inkling who did it and what their next move is going to be."

Rachel left Sarah gawping. She had wanted to talk to Waverley after a quick visit with Marjorie, but as soon as Sarah told her Marjorie was insisting on leaving and Graham had passed her fit, she had wasted valuable time trying to change her stubborn friend's mind.

Once on deck fifteen, Rachel used Marjorie's key card to open her stateroom door. She found a dress and clean underwear and put them in a bag, then took the stairs to deck fourteen and opened the door to the outside where she could get some fresh air on her way to the buffet.

It was dark and cold, the chill penetrating through to her bones. She hugged her cardigan close and walked faster. Hearing a thud and a moan coming from the Lido Deck below, she peered over the internal rails, but saw nothing.

After listening for a few minutes for any further sounds and hearing none apart from music in the distance coming from the many entertainment venues, she shrugged, feeling the cold again, and headed on towards the buffet. A nagging feeling stopped her in her tracks when she got back into the warm interior of the ship. Instead of going inside the buffet, she turned and took the stairs down to the Lido Deck, remonstrating with herself about the stupidity of chasing shadows.

Just one quick look, and then I'll get Marjorie her snack. Rachel braced herself for the chill and the wind as she pulled open the door and stepped outside. The deck was damp with sea spray, as the wind had got up and she increased her speed to get this pointless exercise done.

Remembering she had left the wallet Jason had given her in her room, and she still had a target on her back, she hesitated for a moment before shaking the thought from her mind and heading towards where she imagined she'd heard the muffled groan. Rachel could see nothing and was about to turn back, having proven she was making a fuss over piles of loungers tied up in neat stacks, protecting them from the weather, when a shadow attracted her attention just as the heavens opened to pour driving rain her way.

Scrunching her eyes to focus through the deluge, she headed towards the lounger stacks, walking around the back to where the shadow had caught her eye. There, lying on the floor in a crumpled heap, was a man. Rachel bent down to check on his condition and saw with horror that it was Jo-Jo Falconi.

Adrenaline pumped through her body as she felt for a pulse. The rain lashed in sheets of ice-cold water and she was soaking wet. She ripped open the bag containing Marjorie's clothes and covered Jo-Jo with her friend's dress and jacket before racing to the nearest emergency phone.

Once back with Jo-Jo, Rachel felt for a pulse again. After what seemed like a much longer wait than it actually was, she heard footsteps approaching fast. Bernard and Janet Plover appeared with a stretcher.

"Is he alive?" Bernard asked.

"I thought I felt a pulse," Rachel replied.

Janet knelt down next to Jo-Jo and checked his neck.

"Thank God! You're right, there is a pulse. Let me just check there are no broken bones and we'll get him on the stretcher." Janet worked quickly and efficiently while Bernard lowered the trolley to floor level. He then called in the code blue for medics to meet them in the infirmary.

"Okay, let's move him out," Janet instructed.

Rachel helped get Jo-Jo into a straighter position and they rolled him onto the trolley. Bernard strapped him securely and covered him with a space blanket from his medical bag before raising the trolley.

"I can bring your bags," Rachel offered and the two medics gratefully handed them over, then whisked the trolley towards the nearest entrance. Once inside, they commandeered the first lift stopping at that floor, asking passengers to exit for the emergency.

"Can't you take the next one?" a drunk asked.

"No, sir, we can't. Please leave at once." Bernard lifted his head and stuck his chin out at the much taller man who was shuffled out by his friends. "Unbelievable!" Bernard muttered once the lift doors were closed.

Janet put a card into a slot inside the lift, which Rachel presumed would prevent it stopping on every floor on the way down. The doctor then checked the patient again.

Rachel couldn't see Jo-Jo at all because the medics had buried him in silver foil, but Janet's face told her he was still alive.

Just.

Once they arrived on deck two, Gwen took one end of the trolley and they headed quickly through the medical centre and the double doors leading into the infirmary. Graham was at the ready.

"I think we're going to need the ITU bed," said Janet. Graham nodded, and the team headed to the ventilator bed through a set of double doors at the rear, closing the curtains from inside. Bernard, who had lingered behind, took the medical bags from Rachel and squeezed her shoulder.

"Thanks, Rachel. You may have saved this man's life."

Chapter 25

Marjorie hadn't said a word since Rachel's dramatic arrival. Rachel glanced over at her friend, who had been patiently waiting for her attention. The shivering rippled through her body, slowly at first, but it soon became uncontrollable. She tried to talk through chattering teeth.

"It… it… it's J… J… Jo-Jo, the m… m… man I t… t… told you about."

Marjorie sprang into action, taking Rachel's hand and leading her towards the infirmary bathroom. As if on cue, Raggie appeared. Concern filled his eyes and he gave Rachel a sympathetic smile before turning to her elderly friend.

"Can I help, ma'am… Marjorie?"

"A hospital gown, dressing gown and plenty of towels, please."

Raggie was back in an instant with the items Marjorie had requested. He laid them on a chair in the bathroom.

"I'll get some hot coffee, ma'am."

"Thank you," Marjorie said.

Rachel followed Marjorie into the bathroom and sat herself next to the radiator. Marjorie helped her out of the dripping wet clothes and wrapped her in a huge bath towel while drying her at the same time. She gathered Rachel's drenched long hair on top of her head and wrapped it in another towel. Rachel couldn't hold anything or do much to assist because of the uncontrollable shaking.

"Would you like me to run a hot shower?"

Rachel shook her head, knowing inside her whirring mind that it would help, but she just couldn't face any more water tonight. Marjorie left her for a minute to fetch a mug of hot coffee from the infirmary. Rachel wrapped her hands around the mug, finding the welcome heat soothing.

After around ten minutes, she felt relief as the shivering gradually subsided.

"That's the last time I send you to get me clothes, or food," said Marjorie and they both laughed hysterically.

"What are you two laughing at?" Sarah burst into the bathroom, concern lining her face. Rachel's teeth had stopped chattering and she couldn't help appreciating the moment she and Marjorie had just shared.

"Something Marjorie said, relieving tension, to be honest." Rachel eyed her friend. "How's Jo-Jo?"

"You know it's him, then? Did you see what happened?"

"No. It was only by chance I found him at all. I took the outside route to the buffet to get Marjorie's food and thought I heard a bang followed by a moan. I couldn't see anything, but something told me to go back and take a look."

"Your gut, I suppose," grinned Sarah.

"I like to think it was divine intervention. Anyway, I almost didn't see him lying there…" Rachel's voice trailed off as she recalled the rain and the crumpled form of Jo-Jo lying on the cold deck. She shuddered.

"Minutes later and he'd have been dead, Rachel, so it's a good thing you found him."

"How is the poor man?" Marjorie asked.

"Graham… Dr Bentley says he's had a stroke. He's just about conscious now and stable after being given treatment, but his speech has been affected so he can't tell us what happened."

"Was there anything suspicious?" asked Rachel.

"Not that security could find, but Waverley wants to speak to you. He doesn't want to dismiss foul play because you'd mentioned your worry about the man to me and Jason. The attempted poisoning of Marjorie freaked him out."

"I can't tell him any more than I've told you. I saw nothing suspicious."

"I know, but if you speak to him, it would help to get him out of our hair. He's annoyed that Graham won't let him talk to the patient. Not that he would understand him even if he could."

"Is it a nasty stroke?" asked Marjorie.

"Too early to tell. He'll be airlifted to a specialist unit in Oslo as soon as we dock. The sea's too rough to risk a chopper landing right now, and Graham's satisfied he's stable rather than put more lives—"

"I take it someone's told his wife?" Marjorie interrupted.

"She's with him now. She wants to talk to you as well, Rachel."

"Sounds like they're queuing up, dear," Marjorie chuckled.

"I'm not talking to anyone in a dressing gown. Are you on duty, Sarah?"

"Not now the emergency's over. Do you want me to dash up and get you some clothes?"

"You read my mind. You might need to get Marjorie a fresh set too, I used hers to cover Jo-Jo."

"I'll be back in a jiffy. Raggie's ordered food from the kitchen. You can grab something and speak to Waverley at the same time. They're in Gwen's office."

"I suppose that will make the meeting a tad more bearable," Marjorie sniped.

While Sarah was gone, Rachel downed a second mug of coffee and Marjorie refilled her mug. They chatted some more about how lucky it was Rachel had found Jo-Jo when she did. Rachel finished her coffee at a slower pace, breathing in the fresh aroma. "I feel much better. Thank you, Marjorie. Without you, they might have had another patient on their hands." Rachel hugged the towelled dressing gown she had donned and sipped the latest hot coffee.

Marjorie's eyes lit up as she patted Rachel's hand. "I was a little concerned I might need to call on someone for a moment back there."

"You didn't show it."

"I'm British, dear," Marjorie huffed.

Rachel laughed loudly just as Sarah returned with some clothes for both of them.

"I don't know what's so hilarious. A man nearly dies, and from what Raggie tells me, you weren't in much better shape when you came in."

"Sorry," said Rachel. "You wouldn't get it if I tried to explain now. The moment's gone. Anyway, mother hens, you can both leave me now while I get dressed."

"I'll change in the infirmary then," said Marjorie.

After Marjorie and Sarah left, Rachel donned the jeans and t-shirt Sarah had brought and was pleased to see she'd also thought to bring a hairbrush. She removed the towel Marjorie had put over her hair and used a hairdryer in the small dressing room off the bathroom. Queen Cruises really thought of everything. With hair groomed and dry, and feeling more like herself, she stepped out of the bathroom into the infirmary. There was no sign of Marjorie or Sarah, but Janet raised her head as Rachel walked in. The way she had dealt with Jo-Jo had impressed Rachel, and she could see why Sarah liked the new baby doc so much.

"If you're looking for Sarah and your friend, Marjorie, they're in Gwen's office," Janet told her.

"Thanks, I'll head on through."

"I thought your reputation was a myth, but you really do seem to attract trouble. How do you get through your days alive?"

Rachel wasn't sure how to answer, but when she saw the creases form around the honest brown eyes and the dimples in Janet's cheeks widen as she grinned, she knew she didn't need to.

"If you don't mind me saying, you're an improvement on the last baby doc."

"So I hear. I would have loved to have met her. Was she really as bad as they tell me?"

"Yep. Probably worse."

"I guess the 'Brillo Sin' bit was made up, though, right?"

"Nope. That was her name, and she had the bedside manner of an executioner. Born a few centuries too late, if you ask me."

Janet shook her head, laughing. "Her getting shut in the cupboard, though: surely that bit was made up?"

Rachel shook her head. She liked this new doctor very much.

"On a more serious note," Janet changed the subject, "before you go, I've been looking out for you. Mrs Falconi would love it if you could spare her a minute."

"Of course. Am I allowed in there?"

"Follow me."

Rachel followed Janet into the small intensive care unit. She'd been told about its addition when the ship had been dry-docked several months ago for a refurb, but had never been inside. It was state-of-the-art, with all the equipment she'd seen when waiting for victims to recover, or not, in units in big hospitals as part of her day job.

There was no time to comment. Celia May rushed over, enveloping her in a warm embrace. Rachel held her, looking over her shoulder at the pale Jo-Jo attached to monitors and drips, unconscious but breathing without assistance.

"Thank you so much for saving my husband's life." The older woman released Rachel and held her gaze. "I couldn't live without him."

Rachel wasn't sure what to say. She glanced at Bernard, who was attending the monitors and machines. He gave a fifty-fifty wave of his hand. Jo-Jo didn't waken.

"I was pleased to help. Your husband's a lovely man."

Tears ran down the face that seemed to have aged ten years since their meeting a few days ago.

"This is exactly what I was worried about. It's all my fault: we had a row, but I should have gone after him. When he forgot his stick, I thought he'd come back. We rarely argue, but he had it in his head there was something more to the actor's death and said he was closing in on the killer."

Rachel stiffened, holding back the barrage of questions she wanted to fire at the traumatised woman.

"We argued about it. I was worried about his blood pressure. Our doctor had warned him to take it easy, and I could tell he was getting overexcited."

Rachel couldn't resist one question. "Did he say who he thought the killer was?"

"No." Celia May looked up at Rachel. "He was right, then? There is a murderer out there?"

"Your husband is very perceptive, but I'm sure you already know that." Rachel couldn't see the harm in letting Celia May know her husband was right. He might die, and she would never have the opportunity again to vindicate him in his wife's eyes.

"I guessed he might be. He usually is when it comes to these matters; I just didn't want him involving himself. His health's not what it was. He doesn't sleep well with the pain in his knee. He doesn't complain, but he's in pain most of the time. And now this."

She went back to the chair beside Jo-Jo's bed and held his hand.

"If there is a killer out there, you find him – for Jo-Jo, and for me. He'll want you to." Imploring eyes met Rachel's. "He told me you're a detective on land."

"I'll find the perpetrator. Of that you can be certain," said Rachel, turning back towards the door.

"Rachel?" The quivering voice caused her to pause and turn around.

"Yes?"

"You don't think the killer had anything to do with what happened to Jo-Jo, do you?" She nodded to her husband lying on the bed.

Janet shook her head, warning Rachel to be careful.

"From what I understand, the senior medical officer and Doctor Plover here say Jo-Jo's had a stroke."

"Would the row have brought it on?" Celia May's bottom lip trembled.

"Strokes can happen to anyone, at any time," Janet intervened. "The best thing you can do now is to be with your husband and be a part of his recovery."

Rachel mouthed a thank you to Janet and left the room, the monitors still beeping reassuringly.

She sighed heavily, seeing Waverley standing on the other side of the infirmary doors. Rachel wondered if what she'd feared had happened to Jo-Jo. Could she have warned him earlier? Was it the stress of the case, or was this vicious killer still intent on removing everyone who got too close to the truth? Either way, they had played their part in what had happened to her new friend, and she was more determined than ever to hunt them down.

Chapter 26

Rachel could tell Waverley was struggling to keep calm, especially when Marjorie insisted on directing digs at him.

"Perhaps, Chief, if you could find out who put poisoned water in my room, we might get somewhere."

Waverley exhaled, neck reddening and the inevitable cough preceding his words. "It's not that simple, Lady Marjorie. A kitchen worker who has been with us for ten years left the bottle outside your room. Mario assumed you had put a 'do not disturb' sign up when it was delivered and took it into your room when he found it."

"What does the kitchen steward have to say?" Rachel asked.

"She says the bottle was on a tray with Lady Marjorie's stateroom number on it. She thought the delivery team had missed it and took it up herself."

"So why leave it outside?" asked Marjorie.

"The kitchen worker doesn't hold a universal pass. I have reprimanded her for not following procedure, but she thought she was being helpful and didn't want her colleagues to get into trouble. I don't believe for one moment there was any malicious intent on her part; she has an impeccable record."

"Let me get this straight," said Rachel. "Someone placed a bottle of water containing atropine on a tray marked with Marjorie's room number somewhere that kitchen staff would usually pick up deliveries. Surely that implicates a crew member?"

"Unfortunately not," said Waverley. "There were galley tours yesterday afternoon. Any passenger could have gleaned the information needed to do the deed if they had the desire. Which clearly they did." Waverley shot a sheepish glance Marjorie's way, waiting for the next onslaught.

"Nevertheless, a brazen move by our would-be poisoner." Marjorie must have tired of tormenting the chief. Rachel was pleased.

"Indeed. If the same person carried out the attempt on your life and the murder of Dudley Bates," Waverley held his hand up to bat away a retort from Marjorie, "and I believe it was, then this person is fearless."

"Or arrogant," added Rachel.

"Yes. To commit a murder in front of a packed audience, and then to pull off an attempt at poisoning with all the risks involved, is either ingenious or stupid."

Waverley's confidence appeared to be growing now Marjorie had calmed down.

"One thing has bothered me," said Rachel. "Why put the atropine in water? It's known to be bitter. The killer would know Marjorie would spit most of it out. Unless…"

"Unless what?" asked Marjorie.

"Unless they didn't intend to kill you, at least not on that occasion. Sarah suggested it may have been a warning sent to scare you – and me – off if they'd sussed out we suspected foul play. What if it was a vain attempt to stop us?"

Waverley sat back in his chair. He picked up his own glass of water and inspected it before putting it to his lips, taking a small sip as if to check for poison before a larger gulp.

Gwen, who had eaten with them and now handed coffees around, spoke. "What you say makes sense, Rachel. Atropine or Deadly Nightshade is bitter to taste. Although it could have killed a woman of Marjorie's age even in a small dose if it hadn't been for the pilocarpine eye drops and you dropping by."

"The killer probably thought I'd be with her when she drank it, or the butler would pour it. Who knows? It was still a risk they were willing to take, and Marjorie could have died because of their rashness."

"We've interviewed all the kitchen staff and no-one noticed anything unusual. To be honest, passengers would stand out like a sore thumb down there, so it's odd."

"Unless the person was dressed to blend in," said Rachel.

"What do you mean?" asked Gwen.

"Think about it. Our chief suspect has to be a thespian. Any of the Creations group would have access to clothes, uniforms and all sorts of items they could use as a disguise. Chances are whoever it was donned clothes similar to those worn by your galley staff, disguised themselves with makeup and whatnot, then did the deed, thereby making themselves invisible."

Marjorie's eyes widened. "You've got it, Rachel! We'll never track such a person down."

"There's one hole in your theory, Rachel," said Waverley. "Why risk going into the galley at all? Why not deliver the water to the room themselves?"

Marjorie huffed. "Because, dear chief, you have cameras in the corridors, and even with a disguise, it would be a foolhardy thing to do. Also, they probably wanted to assume the water would be taken into my room, not left in the corridor outside."

The flushing returned to Waverley's neck, spreading up his face. "So we're no further forward, but it explains why no-one from the galley saw anything unusual. Perhaps it's not such a good idea having a bunch of actors on board."

Rachel rubbed her right temple. "Do you have a list of people who attended the galley tours?"

"I'm afraid not. The cruise line lays them on for ad hoc attendance. Passengers line up for a tour, then they're split into groups and a chef heads each group so they can answer questions. We've never identified these tours as a security risk, unlike those to engineering."

"At least we have a direction for our questioning of the cast tomorrow." Marjorie sounded brighter. "We'll ask if any of them have been on galley tours, or whether they know if any of their colleagues – I wouldn't call them friends – did the same."

Waverley coughed. "I'd really rather you and Rachel don't continue investigating. In fact, I'd rather you stayed away from the Murder Mystery Creations company altogether. We can't go along with your plan now, Rachel. It's too risky."

"What you'd rather we do and what we will do are two different things, Chief. And what plan?"

Rachel was relieved to explain. She had felt bad keeping Marjorie in the dark, even if it was for her friend's safety. "I've spread the word I suspect murder via Kate and Enid, and as planned, it got around to all the cast after they told Demos. It's working, Chief, and I don't think we should stop now. My one regret is not warning Jo-Jo – unfortunately, Kate got wind of him being an ex-cop, and no doubt that got around too." She stared down at her hands, noticing they were shaking.

Waverley's mouth dropped open and he rubbed his hand through his hair. Jason arrived at that moment and flopped down onto a chair, saying nothing. Sarah took his hand.

"Now, back to our poor Mr Jo-Jo Falconi. Any thoughts on whether his collapse is related to 'our' investigation?" Marjorie's determined look at Waverley dared him to challenge her. Rachel gave her hand a squeeze.

Waverley fired a few perfunctory questions at Rachel, clearly concerned the killer may have targeted Jo-Jo. She repeated what she'd already told Sarah: she could neither include nor exclude foul play.

"As I'm sure you're aware, the doctors have diagnosed a stroke. When I spoke to his wife before coming here—"

"You spoke to his wife?" Waverley's voice went up several decibels as he glared from Rachel to Gwen.

"Mrs Falconi asked to speak to Rachel. She wanted to thank her for finding her husband and saving his life."

"Humph." Waverley's jaw jutted out.

"If you've quite finished, Chief, perhaps Rachel could finish her story." Marjorie's amusement was evident. She could never resist the opportunity to put Waverley in his place.

"As I was saying," Rachel continued, "when I spoke to Celia May – we met earlier in the cruise, during evening cocktails before dinner one night," she added, noting Waverley's annoyed posture hadn't changed, "she told me her husband believed there was something suspicious about Dudley Bates's death, something he was pursuing, which I'd already gathered—"

"How?" Waverley could usually control himself, but Marjorie must have put him on edge. Couple that with his annoyance at not having been allowed to speak to the Falconis himself, and he was tetchier than usual.

"Calm yourself, Chief. Please allow Rachel to finish." Marjorie chuckled behind her coffee cup.

Rachel looked at Waverley, who nodded for her to continue. She gave a condensed version of her previous conversations with Celia May and Jo-Jo.

"Anyway, he must have found out from Demos that Dudley had in fact died, and tonight he and his wife rowed about him taking it upon himself to investigate. His doctor had warned Jo-Jo to relax because of high blood pressure. He got angry and stormed out to go for a walk. You know the rest of the story."

"High blood pressure's a risk factor for stroke, Jack," Gwen added calmly.

"Humph, something I'm likely to experience first-hand if people keep vital information from me. So at least we can more or less rule out any ill-doing in this case. That's something, I suppose." Waverley's glum expression didn't change, but he sounded calmer. He rubbed his hand through the thinning hair on top of his head and turned to Gwen. "He can't talk, you say?"

"Strokes can cause dysphasia. He can talk, but the condition jumbles his words, so it's not possible for him to put a proper sentence together at the moment. The patient thinks they are saying the words properly, but they come out as something else. Extremely frustrating for them."

"And for anyone needing to know what happened to them," shot back Waverley.

"And that," agreed Gwen.

"How ghastly. Strokes are such dreadful things. I had a cousin who suffered one some time ago." Ignoring Waverley's impatient sigh, Marjorie went on. "Her speech came back, though, at least to the point where she could hold a conversation with only the odd error."

"Yeah. The first few days are key in terms of recovery, which is why we want to get Mr Falconi to a specialist stroke unit first thing. Graham's treated him with a thrombolytic."

"Clot buster?" queried Marjorie.

"Yeah, that's the layperson's term for that type of drug. They now play a major part in early stroke treatment and recovery."

"I don't suppose there's any chance he could recover his speech before the chopper arrives in the morning? I'd still like to interview the man."

"If he does, you'll be the first to know, Chief," said Gwen, standing up. "Now, if you guys will excuse me, I've got paperwork to do before I close up for the night. Janet's on call tonight and Bernard's manning the ITU, so if there's any change, I'll get them to call you."

Waverley coughed. "There has been another development, but in view of the late hour, I wonder if you and Lady Marjorie had better join me and Goodridge in my office first thing in the morning, Rachel?"

"I'll be coming too," said Sarah, clasping Jason's hand protectively.

Waverley shrugged. "As you wish."

"I was going to suggest the same thing," said Rachel. "I'm going to need some information – it can wait, but if I'm right, there will most likely be another murder attempt tomorrow night."

Seeing Waverley's face drop, Marjorie took Rachel's arm.

"Yours, if you're not careful with the chief," she chuckled.

Chapter 27

Rachel surprised herself with how well she slept, considering all she'd been through the night before. Now the sound of the telephone ringing next to her bed woke her with a start.

"Hello?"

"Good morning, Rachel. Sorry to disturb you, but we're about to dock and the chopper's just landed. Mrs Falconi wants to speak to you; she thinks she's got a message from her husband. Are you happy to have a word?" Gwen asked.

"Of course, please put her on."

Rachel heard the phone being passed over and voices in the background speaking Norwegian.

"Rachel, is that you?"

"Yes, hello, Celia May, how's Jo-Jo?"

"He's coming round a lot more and has gotten quite agitated because he can't communicate properly yet. I've managed to work out he wants me to give you a message, but it doesn't make much sense. I promised him I'd try, anyways, and he gave me a thumbs up."

Celia May sounded brighter. Gwen had said the first forty-eight hours following a stroke were vital, and it warmed her heart to hear Jo-Jo was being feisty. It raised her hopes.

"Okay. Try me."

"He keeps repeating words that are jumbled and sound like a mixture of digress, dungeons and dangerous. I can't work out which word he wants me to tell you because he shakes his head when I repeat each one."

Rachel held her head, willing a headache to go away. She took a drink of water.

"And you don't know what any of this means?"

"No, but I'll tell you one thing. The chief medical officer noticed a massive bruise on his leg this morning and he called your security bloke to take a look. It appears someone could have attacked Jo-Jo after all, so you be careful now."

"I will. Would you mind letting me know how he gets on once he's settled?"

"Of course, give me your cell number."

Rachel told her the number and Celia May repeated it back.

The voices got more urgent in the background. "Sorry, Rachel, I have to go. The paramedics are leaving with a doctor from the hospital in Oslo. At least I get to fly in a helicopter for the first time."

"Take care, Celia May, and give Jo-Jo my love. Actually, tell him I think I know what he's trying to say."

"Whether or not that's true, I know it will make him feel better. Thanks again, Rachel, for everything."

The phone went dead and Rachel sat thinking in the darkness for a while, more convinced than ever. She knew who the killer was, but could she convince Waverley when she had so little to go on? She reached for a pack of paracetamol and took two with a glass of water.

***

An hour later, Rachel and Marjorie were sitting around the familiar coffee table in Waverley's office, along with the chief himself, Jason and Sarah. A tray of pastries, toast and croissants arrived shortly after they did, along with three pots of fresh coffee and a pot of tea. It became evident they'd all missed breakfast as they cleared the tray in a matter of minutes.

"Brenda told me you wouldn't have had time to eat," Waverley said.

"Your wife is quite intuitive," said Marjorie. "Please thank her for us for being so thoughtful."

Waverley's eyes brightened in response to the compliment to his wife. "I will. Now, I think it's time to get down to business. I was hoping to dissuade you from continuing to investigate, but after your parting shot last night, Rachel, I feel we'd better hear what you have to say. First, though," he coughed and shot Jason a sympathetic look, "a passenger has gone missing. You may remember Goodridge mentioning another actress called Krystal Brewer?"

Rachel nodded. "Yes, the lady Jason was worried about."

"Was he? Did I miss something?" Marjorie asked.

"It was while you were in the infirmary, Lady Marjorie. Goodridge joined Rachel and Sarah on their tour yesterday."

Jason's head was down. This had obviously hit him hard.

"Oh, I remember now. You mentioned her the other day in the Jazz Bar and we heard a callout for her yesterday before Rachel went out for the evening. What's happened?"

Jason met Marjorie's eyes, his swollen from lack of sleep. "We don't know. I heard she went to Demos Benedict's room three nights ago, and it transpires she hasn't returned to her room since. Her bed hasn't been slept in."

"You don't think she's been—"

Marjorie was cut off. "I don't know what's happened. All I know is that I had a responsibility towards her and I failed. Now she could be dead."

Sarah took Jason's hand and squeezed.

"And have you spoken to Demos about it?" asked Rachel.

"I told him we were looking for a friend of his and asked when he last saw her. He confirmed she was in his room that night. They had a drink and a few laughs as he put it, they discussed what he might do in the future, then she left to play roulette while he went to meet the women you dine with each night, Rachel. We don't have CCTV of her leaving his room because the cameras were down in the Creations corridor until yesterday, but the croupier remembers seeing her and video footage confirms she was there. After that, we pick her up again in the atrium and lose her when she goes up to the open decks. It seems a lot of our cameras have been out recently and haven't been a maintenance priority." Jason's tone was more accusatory than usual.

"Now, now, Goodridge, let's not jump to conclusions. The lady left the ship on both days since then, and returned safely," Waverley explained to Rachel and Marjorie. "Her card was swiped on and off yesterday, and the day before when we were in Stavanger."

"I've been thinking about that, sir, after you told me what Rachel proposed last night concerning the kitchen imposter. What if someone dressed up as Krystal and swiped her card on and off to throw us off the scent? In which case, she could have been kidnapped, or attacked and thrown overboard the night she didn't return to her room."

Waverley's head shot up. "That's absurd! Who would be able to pull off a stunt like that?"

"A very determined killer," said Rachel and Marjorie in unison.

"Skilled in acting," Rachel added.

"But it would have to be a woman."

"I take your point, but not necessarily," said Rachel. "With makeup and wigs and plenty of preparation time, it could be pulled off by a man."

Waverley gulped his coffee, speechless. Marjorie shot him a disapproving look. Jason's sombre mood darkened. He clearly took no pleasure in having had his theory confirmed. Rachel wondered if he'd hoped not to.

"I'll contact port authorities and the captain and explain we have a missing person, but for now that's all she is – missing. Understood? Plus, she's an actress herself. Maybe she's in hiding for some reason. I suggest we continue with the callouts and advise security if someone with her ID tries to swipe off today to stop them."

"Do you still have footage from the casino?" asked Rachel.

"Yes," said Jason.

"Why not check whether she was with someone that evening?"

Jason snatched at the kernel of hope. "I will."

"Now, Rachel, it's time we heard your theory."

"First, what have you discovered about Jo-Jo Falconi's accident? Celia May told me Dr Bentley found a bruise on his leg."

"Ah yes." Waverley frowned. "The good doctor believes someone kicked him before he collapsed and had the stroke. There's a bruise to the back of the leg not consistent with a fall. I've contacted Oslo and asked them to interview him as soon as he's able to communicate. If someone attacked him, he may have seen who left him for dead. We really need to find this person as soon as possible."

Rachel deliberated over whether to tell them about the message Jo-Jo had tried to send her, but she assumed if she mentioned the word dangerous, Waverley would put a stop to her involvement.

"Could you tell me everything you've found out about Cody Spark's history?"

Waverley sighed heavily. "You can't think he had anything to do with the death or these attacks? Sometimes, Rachel, I think you completely miss the mark, and this is one of those times."

"Chief," Marjorie's voice rose, "I'll have you remember you're speaking to someone who has helped you more times than I can count. Please have the courtesy to hear her out."

Suitably humiliated, Waverley looked at Jason to fill Rachel in.

"He's fifty, single, lives in Manchester, works as a vet, no criminal record. He was engaged once, but his fiancée died in a car accident on her way home from his place. He's got an overbearing mother, and that's about it."

"What about the car accident? Was there anything suspicious?"

"Nothing popped up, but we haven't accessed the police files. We'd need permission and it was a while ago; open and closed, as far as we know."

Rachel thought for a moment. "Has he always lived in Manchester?"

"We believe so, yes."

"And is there any evidence Dudley Bates lived in Manchester or that their paths crossed, particularly around the time of the fiancée's death?"

"I see where you're going with this now," said Waverley. "You think there might have been something suspicious about the fatal car accident and Bates knew about it? It's a long shot, Rachel."

Rachel stroked her head, the background headache still making its presence felt. "It's worth looking into. Perhaps Dudley had a fling with the fiancée; we've already found out his relationship with his wife was not exclusive. What if Cody found out about such an affair and wrought his revenge? Then he meets Myra, comes across Dudley Bates again and discovers his new love also had a fling with him. Add this to the worry that Dudley may have suspicions about the fiancée's death. Cody's the quiet, brooding sort.

These types can be the most dangerous of all when they flip. He's also a vet, so presumably he'd know all about atropine. He told Marjorie and me his mother had wanted him to be a doctor."

"So who do you think he's going to kill next?" Waverley asked.

"If it is Cody, Leanne Bates would be a target," Marjorie interjected. "She's the only person left who might know about the affair, if there was one, and her husband's suspicions about Cody's fiancée's death."

"There's a lot of supposition here, but it might be all we have for now. So we need to put in a request for the police report from the road traffic accident, and do an address search to check whether Dudley and Leanne Bates lived in Manchester around the time of the fiancée's death," said Waverley. "Both doable, although we might not get the police report back in time if you really think there will be another murder attempt tonight, Rachel. I'll get on it straight away. Perhaps we could arrest Mrs Bates on suspicion of murder; that would keep her out of harm's way."

"But then we wouldn't catch the killer," Marjorie snapped. "And I want the person who tried to poison me and who attacked that poor man last night brought to justice."

"I still think Leanne Bates is our killer," retorted Waverley.

"Either way, I've got a plan for preventing the potential murder," Rachel said.

Waverley grimaced. "I thought you might have."

Rachel explained what she had in mind for after the last show. She had to give Waverley credit for agreeing to go along with it, despite his misgivings.

Chapter 28

Rachel and Marjorie stayed aboard ship, making preparations for the evening. After they'd eaten lunch, Rachel tasked Marjorie with chatting to Leanne Bates, as the woman had taken an instant dislike to Rachel during her one and only attempt.

"Try to get a bit of background on her, talk about places you've both lived, and mention Manchester."

"I can do that. Better to get it from the horse's mouth, as it were. I don't suppose these address checks are always accurate. Should we speak to Cody again?"

"No, I think we'd best steer clear. If we mention his previous fiancée, we'll set alarm bells ringing."

"What are you going to do?"

"I'll be in the Internet Café carrying out some research. We'll meet up in Creams at three-ish."

"Right. I'll see you then. Should I speak to the mother if she's around?"

"Yes, but stick to the fictional crime unless she opens up on any other level. And whatever you do, don't take drinks off anyone other than crew."

"Understood." Marjorie's eyes sparkled again at being given something to do. What she didn't know was that one of the ship's security guards would tail her the whole time.

Rachel had reluctantly put on the wire and inserted the earpiece so she wouldn't be followed. She switched it on.

"I'll be in the Internet Café, then Creams."

"Okay, see you at three," Jason replied.

Once she got to the cafe, she switched off the transmitter and began her search. Two hours later, she was still engrossed when she checked the time. She signed out and headed to Creams, excited at her finds. The others were already there in the usual quiet spot. Jason's customary upbeat nature was struggling to surface, which most likely meant there was no good news regarding Krystal Brewer.

After ordering drinks and pastries, they got down to business. Sarah opened proceedings.

"Gladys Knott came to surgery this afternoon, feigning one of her funny turns. Her son accompanied her."

Rachel hoped Sarah had raised no suspicions. "And?"

"We got chatting. She was telling me about Cody's engagement to Myra when she noticed the engagement ring hanging around my neck. I can't wear it when working because of infection control." Sarah flushed and exchanged a coy glance with Jason. "To be honest, I was taken aback by how happy she seemed for the couple. Cody beamed throughout and looked adoringly at his mother. It's like she's had a personality change, but…"

"You don't think it's genuine?" Marjorie suggested.

"I feel mean saying it, but I suspected she was acting the entire time. The happiness didn't appear sincere. She's got her son wrapped around her finger, so I guess she's trying to make the best of it rather than alienating her precious boy."

"Who could be a cold-blooded killer," said Rachel.

"Cody said little about the engagement, other than he and Myra would keep it brief and marry in the spring. I asked where they'd be marrying and he said in Manchester. That's all I got out of him. I didn't dare mention anything about his previous engagement; I didn't want to give anything away."

Rachel exhaled, relieved at her friend's discretion.

"There was one awkward moment when I asked if they would live in Manchester. Cody went quiet before saying he and Myra might move to London."

"What did the dragon say to that?" asked Marjorie.

"Nothing. She blanked it as if he hadn't spoken. I got the feeling it won't be the last word on the topic, though."

"I'm certain of it. I have news, too," said Marjorie, hardly able to contain her excitement. "The Bates couple didn't live in Manchester, but they lived on the outskirts for five years from 2005 to 2010."

"Jenny Singh died in a car accident in 2008," said Rachel.

"Was that the name of Cody's fiancée?" asked Sarah.

"Yes… sorry, Marjorie, do continue," said Rachel.

"My less welcome news is that Leanne says she hadn't met Cody until he began dating Myra. I didn't ask whether her husband knew him because it would have seemed an odd question. It doesn't mean he didn't, though."

"My information confirms the Bates' lived in Greater Manchester around that time, but we don't have a police accident report yet. It could take days," said Jason.

"No news on Krystal?" prodded Sarah.

"No. She spent some time chatting to a man in the casino, but they left separately. I'm trying to find out who he is; I'll pop down there later tonight."

"Okay," said Rachel. "So, I tracked down newspapers and found a full-page article on the tragic accident. The reason it attracted local media attention is that Jenny Singh – who was also a vet – was the daughter of a local philanthropist, and it was to be the first mixed-race marriage in the wealthy family's history. Jenny was a popular vet, and partner in a large veterinary practice in the city. Apparently, she and Cody met when two practices were merging. The couple were soon to be wed, according to the newspaper, but for the fateful accident.

"And here's where it gets interesting. The article says police believe she was eating chocolate when she lost control of her vehicle and veered off the road into a ditch. It was late at night and she wasn't found until her colleagues reported her missing after she didn't turn up for work the following day. There was no alcohol in her system, as she didn't drink. The paper reports the news devastated her fiancé, and her family."

"Why's losing control of the car while eating chocolate interesting? Aren't accidents often caused by being distracted at the wheel?" Marjorie asked.

"Yes, but in the light of what we know about this case so far, chocolates are a magnificent vehicle for poisoning, particularly if the box is given to the woman to take home by a killer."

"And was it?"

"Sadly, I don't know, but I suspect so, which still puts Cody in the frame."

"But where's the motive?" Jason asked. "If they were happy, as the article suggests, and the theory about a fling with Dudley Bates seems way off for a woman whose father is a pillar of society, I can't get my head around it. There's got to be something we're missing."

"I can't believe it either, to be honest," said Sarah. "I know you're usually right, Rachel, but this time, I'm not so sure."

They were confirming doubts she'd had herself. "Let's just go along with the plan tonight. At worst, I'll look like an idiot, and at best, we'll prevent a murder. Perhaps the missing piece of the puzzle will emerge during the evening, because I agree with you, Jason, there is one."

"I'm not so sure, Rachel," Jason argued. "I think Waverley might be right about it being Leanne Bates or Demos Benedict."

"It definitely wasn't Demos; I saw footage taken from Jo-Jo's phone of the time of the murder and he's in the clear. If Leanne Bates doesn't know Cody, you could be right, but the news article confirms my suspicions about one thing. My gut tells me that poor young woman was murdered all those years ago, and the killer got away with it then. I don't want to see anyone else come to the same end."

"I guess I can persuade the boss to give it one more night. Your hunches are usually right," said Jason.

***

Rachel sat at the table, heart and head pounding. She had serious misgivings about her theory and could hardly concentrate on what was happening during the performance with her brain in overdrive. Then suddenly, when she was studying the actors on stage, it clicked. It all fell into place.

"I've got it!"

Marjorie nudged her as people from the adjacent table turned to stare. Enid and Kate were too busy ogling

Demos to pay her any attention, and Kate had been particularly rude to Marjorie over dinner.

Rachel whispered to Marjorie, who focused and nodded. The last act ended when the doctor, assisted by the chief of security, entrapped the murderer, who turned out to be the duchess, as she tried to poison her. The dramatic conclusion brought 'Murder on Deck' to an end and the curtain closed to rapturous applause as on previous nights, along with a standing ovation. As Rachel and Marjorie joined in the clapping and cheering, the younger woman stared at one person on the stage with a determined look.

I'm going to wipe that smile off your face, she vowed inwardly.

"I didn't see that coming," remarked Enid.

"Me neither," said Kate. "We thought it was Toni Cleeves, the lounge singer."

"Oh really?" said Marjorie, smugly. "We guessed, didn't we, Rachel?"

"Yeah, right," said Kate, drawing a nudge and a look of warning from Enid.

"Congratulations," said Enid. "What made you think it was her?"

"It was all in the eyes, dear. One can't hide hatred from the eyes." Marjorie's own eyes fixed on Kate's, and Rachel thought how right she was.

After the curtain calls, Tatum took to the stage and Myra placed the box containing the postcards of the guests who had picked the correct murderer in front of her.

"And now's the moment you've all been waiting for. It appears we have several would-be sleuths in this room," she waited for the laughter to subside. "Around a third of you got it right, but there can only be one winner."

Tatum reached into the box after instructing Myra to shake it up and pulled out an envelope. She opened it, removing the card from inside.

"Congratulations go to…" she held the audience in anticipation for longer than necessary, and finally read out, "Lady Marjorie Snellthorpe. Where are you, Lady Marjorie?"

Marjorie stood to an enormous round of applause and some cheers.

"Lady Marjorie, please join us on stage."

Rachel watched proudly as Marjorie made her way to the stage, shaking hands with Tatum, followed by Myra, while clapping rang through the lounge. The only person not happy was Kate, whose bottom lip stuck out as she scowled at the attention Marjorie was receiving. Rachel was beginning to understand why Kate remained single.

After the prize-giving ceremony was over, the curtains closed and Demos approached their table. Ignoring Kate's all too obvious flirtatious giggle, he leaned down towards Rachel.

"Your friend has been invited to stay for celebratory champagne with the cast, and she would like you to join her."

Rachel followed Demos backstage, feeling Kate's eyes boring through the back of her head all the way there.

All good so far.

Chapter 29

Members of cast and crew surrounded Marjorie, congratulating her on her win. Tatum watched on in apparent confusion. A large table was set for the cast and their guests to enjoy a light meal and champagne. Each place had a name card.

Rachel watched the champagne being poured in readiness for when the diners sat down. Her focus remained on one place in particular while members of the cast mingled with their guests. Placing herself next to Marjorie, who remained centre of attention, Rachel observed comings and goings around the table, not taking her eyes off one glass, the object of her attention.

Myra tapped her arm.

"Are you all right?"

"She's fine, just tired and a little star-struck from all the excitement." Marjorie came to the rescue and diverted Myra's attention away from Rachel. Chuckling, Marjorie added, "Young people can't keep up these days; I'm surprised she's not on her phone."

Don't overdo it, Marjorie. Rachel smiled inwardly.

She was beginning to think nothing would ever happen and that Waverley and Jason were right when, at last, she observed a subtle move. A quick sprinkle of liquid and it was over. No-one else noticed; they were all too busy congratulating each other on the end of another successful performance. Technicians were busy packing up equipment and servers were bringing in trays from the galley.

Eventually, Tatum reminded them it was time to take some refreshments and eat. The cast and guests made their way to the places laid out for them. Rachel was seated between Leanne and Myra, while Marjorie was seated between Cody and his mother. Tatum sat next to Demos and Nellie. Rachel gave a nod to Jason and Waverley, who were pretending to be discussing something with the technicians.

Tatum raised a glass. "I propose a toast."

As everyone picked up their glasses, Rachel noticed the triumphant gleam in the poisoner's eye as they watched their target.

"To a successful first performance and many more to follow."

The cast repeated the toast, and each person brought their drinks closer to their mouths. Then Rachel pounced, snatching away a glass.

"I'll take that."

"What the hell?" Myra yelled, startled.

Waverley was behind her in an instant. "I thought Leanne was the target?" he whispered to Rachel.

"Sorry, didn't have time to tell you. It came to me during the performance. Wrong target, wrong killer."

"What are you talking about?" Myra asked, still flustered. "The show's over."

"The fictional one, perhaps, but the real one was just about to reach its climax. Wasn't it, Dr Knott?"

A tableful of wide eyes followed Rachel's gaze. Gladys Knott didn't move an eyelash.

"What's this mad woman talking about, Cody?"

Cody took his mother's hand. "You'd better explain yourself." He looked towards Rachel, his voice rising several octaves to a screech.

Rachel looked up into Waverley's wide eyes. Then he grinned.

"Go for it, it's your show now."

"I'm sorry to be the one to tell you, but this is all about your mother not wanting you to marry any woman on God's earth. The champagne glass Ms Slade was about to drink from has been laced with Deadly Nightshade, a poison your mother is familiar with as atropine from her work as a neurologist."

"This is preposterous!" shouted Gladys. "You, young woman, are clearly deranged."

"Why don't you drink it, then?" Rachel placed the glass in front of Gladys to gasps from the assembled party.

"Not if it might be poisoned. That doesn't mean I put the poison there; you could have done it, for all we know."

"I watched you do it." Rachel's gaze was unflinching, but she had to hand it to the doctor: Gladys was in line for an Oscar.

"Cody, I'm tired. I'd like to go to bed now."

Cody dropped his mother's hand as though he'd been electrocuted.

"Tell me this isn't true, Mother."

Gladys glared at Rachel, maintaining a steely gaze.

"Prove it."

"We'll get to that shortly, but first we need to talk about the murder on boarding night."

"What murder?" shouted Nellie. "Did she kill my Dudley?"

"May I remind you he wasn't your Dudley, he was mine," Leanne snarled, indifferent to the latest revelation.

Nellie huffed.

Rachel continued, "Yes, Dudley Bates was murdered. I couldn't work out why at first, which is why you weren't on the radar, Gladys, but now I realise that was the whole point: a trial run to see if Dr Frankenstein here could get away with murder. She almost did, but we worked it out, and the post-mortem proved it. So we were onto it being murder from the beginning. She also tried to poison my friend, Lady Marjorie, here. How she found out we were looking into Dudley's death, only she can answer."

Further gasps and a lot of head shaking and open mouths faced Rachel as people listened intently.

"But that wasn't the end. Oh no, she then attacked an elderly man who was also onto her, but unbeknown to her, he survived." Rachel looked up at Waverley. "It was Jo-Jo who put me on to her. His wife gave me a message before they airlifted him to hospital. She said he was trying to warn me of something, but the words were muddled. She thought he was saying digress, dungeon or dangerous. I clicked tonight over dinner as I watched the hatred in this woman's eyes. He was trying to say duchess."

"Of course," said Marjorie.

Rachel now fixed a sympathetic gaze on Cody. "I'm afraid your mother is an obsessional woman. Her masterplan was for Myra to 'accidentally' die here this evening in front of all these guests, sparing no thought for how that would make you feel. She has tried to remove everyone who stood in her way throughout the cruise."

"But she didn't count on our cruise ship sleuth here," said Jason proudly.

"But I was engaged before." Tears welled up in Cody's eyes.

"Yes, and your fiancée met with a tragic accident after being given a box of chocolates. Who gave her the chocolates, Cody?"

Cody's eyes widened as tears ran down his face. He turned towards his mother.

"You're a monster."

"Cody, stop! I've always been there for you, looked after you. They can't prove any of this."

"Ah, but we can." Waverley stepped in. "We kept the video rolling, paying particular attention to this table. I think you'll find we have all the evidence we need, plus we have an eyewitness. Rachel here is an off-duty police officer whose word carries significant weight."

"I suspect you'll also find additional evidence in her handbag," Rachel added.

Gladys's fiery eyes burned towards Rachel before she turned to plead with her son.

"No-one can take care of you like I can. This woman doesn't love you the way I do. I did it for you, for us." She reached out for his arm.

Cody shook her away, turning his back on her. "Please, get her out of my sight."

"With pleasure," replied Waverley. "Goodridge, take her away."

"Just one more question," Jason said. "What did you do to Krystal Brewer?"

"I don't know any Krystal Brewer, unless you mean the mad person who put a threatening note under my door."

"That would be her," Jason confirmed.

"I never met the person."

"She's telling the truth this time," said Demos. "Krystal popped in to see me earlier, told me she'd fallen in with a theatre director and has been staying with him for the past few days. When I told her you were looking for her, she said she'd come down at the next announcement. She was worried maybe the 'fake' actress had found out who she was."

Jason's wide grin filled the room. "Right, Dr Knott, I have just the room for you. You can enjoy the comforts of a ship's brig until we hand you in to the port authorities in Southampton."

"Cody, I don't feel well," Gladys tried again to reach out to her son.

"Mother, I couldn't care less." Myra took his hand as Jason took Gladys Knott away.

Marjorie sipped her champagne before addressing Tatum.

"I suppose you'd better inform the real winner of the competition now."

"You mean this was all a setup?" Myra asked as Cody enveloped her in his arms.

"Well acted! We do have a vacancy for an older actress now," quipped Nellie.

Marjorie raised her hand in protest. "No, thank you. Rachel and I are on holiday from this moment." As she took Rachel's arm and they left together with Waverley, they heard Demos speak up.

"I have just the person to fill that gap, Myra. A Mrs Krystal Brewer."

"Jason will be pleased to hear that," chuckled Marjorie.

Rachel's phone pinged with text messages. The first was from Carlos.

"Found the girl safe and sound, driving her home. Will ring you in the morning."

The second was from an unknown number.

"Jo-Jo here. I'm doing well. It was a nasty mini stroke. The doctors call it a TIA complicated by a touch of hypothermia, should make a full recovery thanks to you. By the way, if you haven't worked it out already, it was the duchess."

Rachel beamed at the phone.

"Good news?" asked Marjorie.

"The best news: Carlos found the missing girl and Jo-Jo's going to make a full recovery," said Rachel.

"That warrants a celebration."

"It does. Now, what say we go meet Sarah in the Jazz Bar?"

"Sorry, I have to work," said Waverley.

"I don't think we invited you, Chief," giggled Marjorie.

Waverley coughed. "Goodnight, ladies."

"Goodnight, Chief," they uttered in unison.

THE END

Author's Note

Thank you for reading *A Murder Mystery Cruise*, the eighth book in my Rachel Prince Mystery series. If you have enjoyed it, please leave an honest review on Amazon and/or any other platform you may use. I love receiving feedback from readers.

Keep in touch:

Signup for my no-spam newsletter and receive a FREE audiobook of the first-in-series. You will also receive news of new releases, special offers and have the opportunity to enter competitions.

Join now:

https://www.dawnbrookespublishing.com

Follow me on Facebook:

https://www.facebook.com/dawnbrookespublishing/

Follow me on Twitter:

@dawnbrookes1

Follow me on Pinterest:

https://www.pinterest.co.uk/dawnbrookespublishing

Books by Dawn Brookes

Rachel Prince Mysteries

A Cruise to Murder

Deadly Cruise

Killer Cruise

Dying to Cruise

A Christmas Cruise Murder

Murderous Cruise Habit

Honeymoon Cruise Murder

A Murder Mystery Cruise

Hazardous Cruise (Coming Soon, 2021)

Carlos Jacobi PI

Body in the Woods

The Bradgate Park Murders (Preorder Now)

Memoirs

Hurry up Nurse: memoirs of nurse training in the 1970s

Hurry up Nurse 2: London calling

Hurry up Nurse 3: More adventures in the life of a student nurse

Picture Books for Children

Ava & Oliver's Bonfire Night Adventure

Ava & Oliver's Christmas Nativity Adventure

Danny the Caterpillar

Gerry the One-Eared Cat

Suki Seal and the Plastic Ring

Acknowledgements

Thank you to my editor Alison Jack, as always, for her kind comments about the book and for suggestions, corrections and amendments that make it a more polished read. Also thanks to Alex Davis for the final proofread.

Thanks to my beta readers for comments and suggestions, and for their time given to reading the early drafts. A special thank you to Margaret Grain, one of my readers who suggested the name Nellie Hurst.

Thanks to my immediate circle of friends who are so patient with me when I'm absorbed in my fictional world and for your continued support in all my endeavours.

I have to say thank you to my cruise-loving friends for joining me on some of the most precious experiences of my life, and to the cruise lines for making every holiday a special one.

About the Author

Dawn Brookes holds an MA in Creative Writing with Distinction and is author of the *Rachel Prince Mystery* series, combining a unique blend of murder, cruising and medicine with a touch of romance. Her new series involving a tenacious PI may also be of interest to fans of Rachel Jacobi-Prince.

Dawn has a 39-year nursing pedigree and takes regular cruise holidays, which she says are for research purposes! She brings these passions together with a Christian background and a love of clean crime to her writing.

The surname of Rachel Prince is in honour of her childhood dog, Prince, who used to put his head on her knee while she lost herself in books.

Bestselling author of *Hurry up Nurse: memoirs of nurse training in the 1970s* and *Hurry up Nurse 2: London calling*, Dawn worked as a hospital nurse, midwife, district nurse and community matron across her career. Before turning her hand to writing for a living, she had multiple articles published in professional journals and coedited a nursing textbook.

She grew up in Leicester, later moved to London and Berkshire, but now lives in Derbyshire. Dawn holds a Bachelor's degree with Honours and a Master's degree in education. Writing across genres, she also writes for children. Dawn has a passion for nature and loves animals, especially dogs. Animals will continue to feature in her children's books, as she believes caring for animals and nature helps children to become kinder human beings.